NEST OF

Gladys Maude Winifred Mitchell – or 'The Great Gladys' as Philip Larkin called her – was born in 1901, in Cowley in Oxfordshire. She graduated in history from University College London and in 1921 began her long career as a teacher. She studied the works of Sigmund Freud and attributed her interest in witchcraft to the influence of her friend, the detective novelist Helen Simpson.

Her first novel, *Speedy Death*, was published in 1929 and introduced readers to Beatrice Adela Lestrange Bradley, the heroine of a further sixty six crime novels. She wrote at least one novel a year throughout her career and was an early member of the Detection Club, alongside Agatha Christie, G.K Chesterton and Dorothy Sayers. In 1961 she retired from teaching and, from her home in Dorset, continued to write, receiving the Crime Writers' Association Silver Dagger in 1976. Gladys Mitchell died in 1983.

VINTAGE MURDER MYSTERIES

With the sign of a human skull upon its back and a melancholy shriek emitted when disturbed, the Death's Head Hawkmoth has for centuries been a bringer of doom and an omen of death - which is why we chose it as the emblem for our Vintage Murder Mysteries.

Some say that its appearance in King George III's bedchamber pushed him into madness. Others believe that should its wings extinguish a candle by night, those nearby will be cursed with blindness. Indeed its very name, *Acherontia atropos*, delves into the most sinister realms of Greek mythology: Acheron, the River of Pain in the underworld, and Atropos, the Fate charged with severing the thread of life.

The perfect companion, then, for our Vintage Murder Mysteries sleuths, for whom sinister occurrences are never far away and murder is always just around the corner …

GLADYS MITCHELL

Nest of Vipers

VINTAGE BOOKS
London

Published by Vintage 2014

2 4 6 8 10 9 7 5 3 1

First published in Great Britain by
Michael Joseph Ltd in 1979

Vintage
Random House, 20 Vauxhall Bridge Road,
London SW1V 2SA

www.vintage-books.co.uk

Addresses for companies within The Random House Group Limited
can be found at: www.randomhouse.co.uk/offices.htm

The Random House Group Limited Reg. No. 954009

A CIP catalogue record for this book
is available from the British Library

ISBN 9780099583998

The Random House Group Limited supports The Forest Stewardship
Council® (FSC®), the leading international forest-certification organisation.
Our books carrying the FSC label are printed on FSC®-certified paper.
FSC is the only forest-certification scheme supported by the leading
environmental organisations, including Greenpeace. Our
paper procurement policy can be found at
www.randomhouse.co.uk/environment

Printed and bound by Clays Ltd, St Ives PLC

CHAPTER 1

Unexpected Legacy

(1)

Claud Rufford, of Cox, Cox, Rufford and Cox, sat impassively on a hard chair watching his client who was walking to and fro, reminding him of one of the larger cats at the London Zoo.

'So there it is,' said the client, 'and how I'm going to get out of it I simply haven't a clue.'

'We've briefed the best man in Britain,' said the solicitor. 'Sir Ferdinand works wonders with a jury.'

'He'll need to work miracles,' said the caged leopard, coming to a halt. 'I've been framed. I know I've been framed, but I can't put a finger on the criminal. I've been over and over in my mind—'

'Sir Ferdinand wants you to write everything down.'

'What's the good of that? I've already made a statement.'

'His mother is the Home Office psychiatrist.'

'Good Lord! I'm not a mental case.'

'Dame Beatrice is also a noted criminologist. She has solved dozens of cases in her time. Sir Ferdinand believes your story and he thinks that a written account, apart from any statement you may have made to the police, might bring out details which would suggest something to Dame Beatrice. You are a novelist, so the writing shouldn't present any difficulty from your point of view. I need not advise you not to embroider your account. She can detect a lie or an exaggeration as though it literally stinks.'

'I've been over the whole thing, first with the police and then with you. There is nothing I can add. I've told the truth and there's no more to be said.'

'Very well, but I think it's short-sighted of you to ignore advice. And I don't need to tell you that we've very little ammunition at present.'

'Oh, well, it will help to while away the time, I suppose, if I write an unofficial version.'

'Good man. I'll have writing materials sent in. All the details, mind. Treat it as though it was part of your next novel, except that it will be solid fact, not fiction.'

(2)

I have been told to tell you everything, Dame Beatrice, so here goes. It began when I came into money and property by one of those freakish decrees of fortune which make truth so much more unlikely than fiction. I was young, ambitious and, at the time, profoundly dissatisfied with my lot, too poor to marry and hating my bread-and-butter job which did not leave me enough leisure to do the thing I badly wanted to do. Like so many young men who have had a university education, I wanted to write.

One January morning I read a newspaper advertisement of a trip to Madeira by passenger-cargo boat. The fares quoted seemed reasonable so I sent for the brochure, made an assessment of my savings and decided that, by careful budgeting, I could just about afford the lowest price for accommodation on the cruise.

I wrote off at once and secured a berth for the following July. The ship, a vessel of four thousand tons, left from Liverpool carrying a mixed cargo. Eighty passengers were taken and the only amenities on board were one deck tennis court, shuffleboard, deck golf, quoits, a canvas tank big enough to allow one to swim a couple of yards and a small, tatty library, and even this had to be housed in a smoking-room cum bar which also did duty as the only lounge.

In spite of the simplicity, almost the austerity, of the arrangements, I think we enjoyed ourselves. Most of us were young and, except for a middle-aged lady who occupied the so-called *de luxe* cabin amidships and, on the strength of this, reserved for her exclusive use the only deck-shelter available, I suspect that the others had had to save money for the holiday, just as I had, and needed to watch their holiday spending rather anxiously.

The ship was to stay thirty-six hours off Madeira, but,

before we could be taken ashore, the cargo for the port of Funchal had to be landed. We were anchored out in the bay and for some time our amusement was provided by bumboatmen and diving-boys who came out to the ship in their own little craft and touted vociferously for our spare cash.

After they had returned to the quay, our crew let down the passenger ladder so that we could be taken ashore. The water was so calm and clear that, as the diving-boys had demonstrated, you could see a coin lying on the sand at a depth of thirty feet.

I approached the deck steward and asked whether there was time for a swim before we went ashore. He replied that there was about an hour before the ship's boats would be leaving. He warned me that the water was deeper than it looked. Soon all of us who could swim were in the water, and so was our cabin *de luxe* passenger, who, although she could manage one or two floundering strokes, was not, in my sense of the words, a swimmer.

Whether the clearness of the water deceived her as to its depth, whether she did not realise that water deep enough to float a ship, even one of our tonnage, was too deep for her to be able to put her feet down when she was tired, I do not know. Suddenly she panicked, and got a mouthful of water as she submerged. However, I had no difficulty in getting her back to the safety of the ship's ladder, on to which she was hauled by one of the sailors.

I thought no more of the matter, but after we had returned from the shore excursion she sought me out and thanked me – for 'saving her life'. I replied modestly and sincerely that I had done nothing of the kind. I was the manager of my local swimming pool and accustomed to keeping an eye on people in the water. That, I supposed, was the end of it, for she took no more notice of me for the remainder of the cruise, although the purser, issuing tickets for the shore excursion at Lisbon on the return voyage, did tell me that she had asked for my home address and that he hoped it had been all right to let her have it.

'Not that I should have dreamed of it, had the situation been reversed, of course,' he said.

'You mean if I'd been a blushing maiden and she a lascivious old man? Glad to hear it,' I retorted.

So that was that – or so I thought – for I heard nothing more until, nearly five years later, the letter came from her lawyers. I had been left a considerable house standing in its own grounds and a very substantial sum of money.

My first thought, when I had recovered from the shock of discovering that I had become a landed proprietor and a wealthy man, was that now I should have to marry Niobe. It came as a surprise to me to discover that I no longer wanted to do this. I had come to take our six-year understanding for granted. It seemed to satisfy both of us, although we had never lived together in the accepted sense. Perhaps I had better explain this.

When I left the university with an undistinguished honours degree I tried for work in a publisher's office and then with a literary agency, but found no takers. I was not at all keen on working in an ordinary commercial office, the Civil Service or a bank, let alone becoming a schoolmaster, so I answered an advertisement for superintending and managing a municipal swimming pool. As I held the A.S.A. gold medal and had swum the Channel (although in nothing like record time) they gave me the job.

Niobe Nutley, some few years older than myself, was my opposite number on the women's side and we soon established an easy, comradely relationship. The work was hard and the hours long. I did not much care for the job and the money was nothing much, but, of course, I could swim free of charge every day, which at least was something.

I got digs with a landlady who mothered me, so that I was given plenty to eat, a decent, clean, comfortable bed and no embargo was placed on female or, indeed, any other visitors. I was an orphan, so I was unembarrassed by parental visits or the need to go home at holiday times, and my most frequent guest was Niobe, so we drifted into an understanding that, as soon as my finances warranted such a step, we would marry.

How this arrangement came about I hardly know. She was a good comrade and a loyal second-in-command at the pool, but if there ever had been the beginnings of a passionate relationship between us, I cannot remember when it was. The years came and went – six of them altogether – and any first fine careless rapture must soon have passed. All the same, until my unexpected rise to affluence came about, the mirage of our ultimately getting married was still on the horizon. It was with that perceptiveness which nature, I suppose, has given to women and which is often miscalled their intuition, that, when I told her of my good fortune, Niobe said, living up to her name and becoming tearful:

'So now you won't want me any more.'

I was completely disconcerted by this, for it brought home to me the realisation that she was right. If this seems the reaction of a heel, I'm sorry, but it must be remembered that she and I had had nothing but the most undemanding kind of relationship for at least five years. We had never slept together and, owing to the nature of our jobs, we had never, even at the warmest period of our friendship, spent a holiday together. One or other of us always had to be on duty at the pool, for a deputy could never be placed in full control of the swimming. That was in our contract and the agreement had to be honoured.

Recovering from my surprise at finding that she had hit a nasty smash, with almost uncanny accuracy, straight at my head, unchivalrously I lobbed the ball back into her court.

'You mean that *you* don't want *me* any more,' I said. My excuse for saying this was that, now it had come to the crunch, I hoped that maybe she had stuck to me so long merely for the sake of Auld Lang Syne and might be as glad as I was to get out of the entanglement. I had great hopes that for at least the past three years her feelings for me had become as tepid as mine for her and that she was relieved to find a way of escape.

'I don't want you any more?' she asked, wiping her eyes on a used bath towel she had been about to toss into the bin. 'Well – ' she put on the affected American drawl which she thought funny but which secretly irritated me very much – 'I guess I never figured on being a rich man's wife. Anyway, what do you plan to do now?'

I had already made up my mind about this.

'I shall give in my notice at the pool,' I said, 'and as soon as I have worked out my month I shall go to Paris and write my novel.'

'Won't you live in the house this woman has left you?'

'No. It is far too large. Unfortunately it needs a great deal done to it before I have any hope of selling it, but all that can wait.'

'I don't want to go to Paris,' said Niobe. I suppose I looked taken aback. It had not occurred to me to suggest that she should accompany me. That would be no way to break our liaison.

'Oh, I see,' she added at once. 'No doubt I should be in the way.'

'It isn't that,' I said, 'but, well, I shall be pretty busy with my writing, you know. I mean, there wouldn't be shopping and the opera and the *Folies* and all that sort of thing. It wouldn't be any fun for you. Besides, there's your job. One of us has to stay here in charge of the pool. You wouldn't want to— what I mean is that I shall only be gone for a year. I don't intend to live permanently in Paris.'

'All right, all right,' she said. 'I've told you I don't want to go with you. No need for all these excuses. Anyway, if all I hear about Paris is true, you'll want to feel perfectly free to go all Montmartre there, so perhaps you'd better have this back.'

She took off the ring I had given her five years previously. At the pool she did not wear it on her engagement finger, but on the forefinger of her left hand.

'Oh, come, now!' I said, nonplussed by her definite reaction. 'No need for histrionics. A year is only a year. I shall be back again almost before you know I've gone. We can make all our arrangements then.'

'Very well,' she said. It was clear to me that she had herself in hand, for she put the ring back, but this time on to her right hand. There was not going to be any fuss. She smiled brightly at me, but added, to my dismay, 'Just so long as you don't plan to be shut of me altogether. Why don't you take me to see this ducal mansion of yours? It's good for the poor to see how a rich man lives.'

'I'm not going to live there, I tell you,' I said, exasperated by what seemed a *volte-face* on her part, 'and I can't take you to see it until I've worked out my notice and we can use your half day.'

'Don't you want me to see it?'

'Yes, of course I do, if you'd like to. Not that you'll think much of it in its present state. It will take thousands to do it up. I wonder really whether it wouldn't be better to let it maunder into total decay rather than spend all that money on it and then perhaps not be able to sell it.'

(3)

When I had visited my acquisition in company with my benefactor's lawyer, I had not been surprised when, as we went in through the great iron gates, he said:

'Of course, Mrs Dupont-Jacobson never lived here after her husband died. She thought the house was unlucky. A superstitious woman in some ways.'

Paint was peeling off the window-frames, a once-ornate portico was battered and damaged and some of the downstair windows were broken. The whole place was grimy and neglected. All the same, a certain grandeur still clung to it in its decay and it was possible to see that, in its day, it had been a fine, generously-built house.

'A lot will have to be done before I can sell it,' I said. I had made the same remark to Niobe earlier, and I made it again as she and I stood on its front lawn. She made a statement which the lawyer, perhaps, had been too tactful to utter.

'You'll never sell a place this size, Chelion, however much you do to it,' she said.

'A school, perhaps, or a nursing-home might buy it,' I hazarded.

'I doubt whether it's suitable for either. I suppose you've got a key? Let's go inside,' she said.

The interior of the house told the same story as the outside had done. The whole place needed not so much redecorating as renovating. There was a noble staircase with cobwebbed banisters and a grimy sidewall on which had been painted a *trompe l'oeuil* effect in imitation of the banisters themselves, but which was now picked out with a coat of depressing dark brown, peeling paint, and the whole mansion had the same depressing effect on me.

An upstair room in the shape of a double cube with what must have been a wonderfully ornate Jacobean ceiling before smoke from the enormous open fireplace had blackened its coloured splendours opened into an ante-chamber which, like the other rooms on the first floor, had hideous Victorian wallpaper and a nasty little iron fire-grate which ruined its otherwise spacious attractiveness. As well as this, cracked and broken windows had allowed the elements to do their worst, apparently for years, and water seemed to have come through the ceiling. The other rooms were similarly affected.

We tried the second floor, climbed to the attics and, when we had descended to the ground floor again, explored what must have been the housekeeper's room, the butler's pantry and the servants' hall. We inspected the enormous kitchen and its scullery and then returned to the entrance hall with its stone screen and the dado made up of the coats of arms of previous owners.

'I'd have to spend thousands,' I said again, 'even to make it habitable.'

'I know exactly what I should do with it if it were mine,' said Niobe.

'Pull it down and sell the park for building land? I doubt whether I'd be allowed to do that.' I was glad to find her ready to talk rationally about the house and what I was to do with it. She had maintained what I took to be a grim silence up to this point. She had not even lived up to her name and wept. She was much given to tears when things went wrong.

'No, I don't think you would be allowed to sell the park for building plots,' she went on. 'There would be planning permission to get, and all sorts of involvements, I expect, and you never were much of an organiser, were you? No, I can tell you what to do with it, Chelion. In fact, I could do it all for you while you're in Paris. I don't want to stay on at the pool. It won't be the same without you.'

I was afraid she was going to turn tearful at this, so I said hastily. 'Well, you can't expect me to go on with a job like that, now I've no necessity to earn a living, but tell me what you've got in mind, however crazy it is.'

'You'd have to pay me a salary, of course,' she said, 'but I'd be satisfied with the same money as I'm getting at the pool.'

'Let's hear this crack-brained scheme of yours.' But, when she outlined what it was, I said, 'Good Lord! That will never work!'

'Of course it will work. You'll get masses of tenants in no time. There will be a waiting-list. Elderly people who've sold

up houses which are too big for them will give anything for
accommodation they can rent instead of having to buy. There
is the park for them to walk or sit about in, a lake you can
stock with fish, a seaside town and its shops close at hand—'

'Only close at hand if you've got a car. Elderly people may
not be prepared to drive.'

'Well, get a car. Get two cars, one self-drive and the other
chauffeur-driven and charge car-hire prices. They would more
than cover the chauffeur's wages.'

'Each flat would need its own kitchen and bathroom.'

'I know that. Look, why don't you leave everything to me,
as I've suggested? I'm sure I can manage. I'll be able to give a
good account of my stewardship, I promise you. Now we've
– how does it go? – said goodbye for ever, cancelled all our
vows, done our best and worst and parted, and all that, there
could be so easy a relationship between us.'

'Oh, look here,' I said, 'what vows have we cancelled?'

'Don't be silly, Chelion. Will you let me do as I suggest?'

'Perhaps,' I said. 'I'd have to put a ceiling on what I could
allow you to spend, though, you know. I'm no Soames Forsyte
to be employing an architect for whom the sky's the limit.'

'I'll get plenty of estimates and then, when we reach your
ceiling-price – although I hope you won't be niggardly – I
shall stop the work. If necessary, we'll finish it ourselves when
you come back.'

'You can count me out on that score. Interior decorating is
well beyond my scope. I've always known it. Oh, well, get your
estimates and then we'll see,' I promised. After all, I owed her
something for having been engaged to her during the years
when, I suppose, she could have found somebody who would
have married her, and I was grateful, too, for the calm way she
had accepted the break-up. She must have read some of my
thoughts, not an unusual state of affairs, because our friendship, if such it can be called, had lasted so long. She said,
without bitterness:

'You need not think you have wasted the best years of my
life.' She said it with a lop-sided smile. 'Nothing of the kind.
Life begins at thirty, Chelion.'

'Not for a woman,' I thought. On impulse I kissed her, but
met with no response. What is more, she remained dry-eyed.

CHAPTER 2

Nest of Vipers

(1)

So, by the time I got back from Paris, all the alterations had been completed, the repairs and the interior and exterior decorations had been done and my first batch of tenants had been installed. Niobe had managed to turn the house into ten flats and of these only two were unoccupied.

The renovations surprised and pleased me very much, but the inhabitants of my newly-furbished property pleased me a great deal less. Niobe had prophesied that there would be tenants, but those I found in possession of my house were ludicrously different from any I might have envisaged.

I had thought of a retired naval or military man, a wealthy widow or two, a well-known actor or actress 'resting' between shows but still well able to afford the rent of a flat on my well-situated property, a business man still keen on a round or two of golf, a couple well-heeled enough to afford a spacious apartment while they waited to get possession of a house they were buying, and perhaps a wealthy recluse happy to find peace and security far from the madding crowd. Instead of these comfortable, predictable types, all my tenants turned out to be *writers* of one sort or another.

'I thought you'd feel more at home with them, being a writer yourself,' said Niobe. 'Birds of a feather, and all that, you know.'

'Birds of a feather can peck one another to death,' I said, 'and these aren't even "of a feather". What has Evesham Evans in common with Constance Kent?'

'They happen to be a respectable married couple, although I can't think why she chose the pen-name of Constance Kent,' said Niobe, going off at a tangent, as women will.

'Oh, *I* can,' I said. 'The instinct for self-martyrdom is strong in some people. She probably sees Constance Kent, the real one, as her *alter ego.*'

'Constance Kent was a murderess.'

'Nonsense! She decided to carry the can for her father.'

'I won't argue with you. I am certain to get the worst of it. What have you against these people?' Niobe's voice had become slightly shrill and, as so often, there were tears in her eyes. 'What's wrong with them, I say?'

'Nothing at all, provided they pay their rent and behave themselves,' I said, weakly giving ground.

'Why shouldn't they?' Her tone still had a sharp edge. Apparently I was supposed to approve her choice of tenants.

'I have no idea. I'll take your word for them,' I said.

'Well, then!'

'Oh, let it go,' I said.

(2)

As I had told Niobe, I had never intended to live in the house. A bachelor flat in Mayfair, with a manservant to cook, clean and act as my valet (a romantic dream engendered by the stories of P.G. Wodehouse) had been the target on which I had set my sights. When I saw the apartment which Niobe had set aside for me, I changed my mind.

This apartment was on the ground floor and comprised the entrance hall and its noble Jacobean staircase, together with two large, handsome rooms, one of which had an overmantel carved by Grinling Gibbons.

Niobe had contrived a luxurious bathroom for me in what had been the garden-room of the original mansion, the room, that is to say, where the cut blooms were placed ready to be sorted over so that a choice could be made for the drawing-room and dining-room vases. There was no kitchen as part of my flat, although everybody else had one, but when I pointed this out to Niobe she had a ready answer. My meals were to be cooked in the kitchen of the original owner and were to be served in a little dining-room Niobe had contrived out of what had been the game larder. A resident cook was already installed and she and her kitchenmaid had bedrooms up in the attics.

'You can afford it, can't you?' said Niobe. 'You and I will eat together. To share your cook will be one of my perks. I've gone to a great deal of trouble on your behalf, you know. In return I expect free board and lodging and the same pay as I was getting at the pool. I am prepared to run this place for you. Everything will go like clockwork. I've found my *métier*.'

The idea of having her permanently round my neck appalled me. For three meals a day I was doomed, it seemed, to sit at table with her and, apart from this, to me, most undesirable propinquity, it meant that the meals would be served at regular and stated times. I attempted to hedge.

'I don't think the mealtimes will work,' I said. 'I can't be tied down to regular hours like that. No writer can.'

'You have only to say you're working,' said Niobe. 'I can manage the kitchen staff, you'll find.'

There seemed no more to be said. Short of turning her out of the house altogether and sacking the cook and the kitchen maid and foraging for myself (which would be a more serious interruption of my writing than sitting down to regular meals with Niobe) there was no self-assertive attitude I could take.

'Now I'll show you *my* quarters,' she said blithely. 'Are we agreed upon my wages?'

'They are not exactly excessive. You might have done better if you had brought a breach of promise case!' I laughed as I said it, but she remained grave.

'That isn't a nice thing to say, Chelion. You *must* know there could never be any question of that. I have my pride and *some* self-respect.'

Her own apartments were also on the ground floor. She had converted what had been the housekeeper's dayroom, the butler's pantry and the servants' hall into a very cosy little flat which she showed me with pride. What pleased me less, since it brought her into closer contact with my own little realm than I deemed advisable, was that she had allocated to herself as an office – 'I must have a room to which they can come to pay their rent and bring their complaints, Chelion' – the room to the right of the front door opposite to that which I had decided to use as my library and study. However, since she was willing – eager, in fact – to take the whole running of the venture off my hands, it seemed unreasonable to cavil at what was, after all, a perfectly sensible arrangement, so I assented to it without argument except to query the word *complaints*.

'What the hell would they have to complain about?' I asked.

'One another, mostly, I expect,' said Niobe composedly. 'Did you ever know a collection of writers who didn't hate each other's guts?'

'I don't know a collection of writers.' It was true. In spite of my year in Paris, I had not finished my novel, let alone sold it, and therefore I was not eligible to join any literary society except a local one which did not expect many of its members to achieve publication unless they paid for it themselves.

As for my tenants, their talents proved to be so various that, with unconscious snobbery (as I see it now), I would hardly have called some of them writers at all, although there is no denying that every one of them did actually write for a living and, what is more, made enough money to pay the rent.

To take them in my own order of importance: at the top of the list came Evesham Evans. He was a not very successful member of the Ernest Hemingway school of fiction and looked and dressed for what he saw as the part. He was untidy, gruff, bluff and self-consciously addicted to the bottle and the four-letter word. When he roamed the grounds in search of inspiration he habitually carried a sporting-rifle over his arm although, except for some grey squirrels and a colony of rooks, there was nothing to shoot in my park. I think he put on an act to bolster up his ego, because his wife earned more than he did.

Next in my order of meritorious authorship came Mandrake Shard. That this was his real name seems open to doubt, but all his letters, both business and personal, were addressed to him under this cognomen. He wrote highly successful spy stories and an occasional play of the same nature for the BBC. He was a mild, almost furtive, tiny little character; he dressed like an undertaker and was a Methodist lay preacher. I went to hear him once and was surprised and immensely (although secretly) amused by his doctrine of hell fire and his promises of a heaven, which seemed a combination of Blackpool on a bank holiday and a recital by a Welsh male-voice choir. There was no doubt, however, of his financial success as an author.

By accident I once saw his royalties statement and was staggered.

Although Evesham Evans's tough novels had their small following, from the money point of view, as I have said, he was less successful than was Constance Kent, his wife. She was a grim, soldierly woman, older, I think, than he was, and, of all things, she specialised in would-be sultry love-stories which, however, remained so definitely within the bounds of an almost Puritan propriety that it might be said of any heroine of hers: 'Kind are her answers, but her performance keeps no day.' However, many women must have found vicarious satisfaction in her work, for once, out of curiosity, I went to the public library for a copy of one of her books and discovered that, although more than a score were in the catalogue, not one was left on the shelves.

We had three other couples on the books, but they came low on my list. I place above them a bachelor whose pen-name was Latimer Targe. He wrote up real-life crimes, especially murders, in a form which the masses could assimilate without effort. Privately I thought of him as *Mr Sunday Papers* and there was no doubt that, although his syntax was shaky and his style deplorable, he was not only readable but, in his obvious affection for his murderers, definitely endearing. I suppose that among all my tenants, he was, perhaps, my favourite, although that is not saying much.

The couples were 'Polly' Hempseed, a light-hearted young man whole real name was Conway. Under his pseudonym, he wrote the sob-stuff page in a woman's magazine. His partner, a down-to-earth and, some would say, unattractive woman a year or two older than her paramour, was called Cassie McHaig and this, I think, was her real name. As it somewhat blatantly suggests, she was a Scot, but, except at moments of excitement or crisis, one would hardly have guessed it from her accent. She was a weekly columnist on one of the West Country papers and wrote forthrightly on such matters as naughty politicians and the even naughtier public services, including such sitting birds as British Rail, the Post Office and the extravagances in public spending. I was sorry for her. Polly had a roving eye.

Then there were the Irelath Moores. He was a poet who lived mostly on a generous allowance from his father, a

Canadian-Irish cattle rancher. Irelath's girl, who was called Sumatra and who came from Bali, wrote (only I always thought that Irelath did the work and she merely signed it) the beauty hints for a glossy monthly. Her photograph, which looked like the reproduction of a picture by Sir Gerald Kelly, always appeared at the top of her column and was the best advertisement which could ever have been conceived to bear witness to the veracity of her claim to be a beauty specialist. She was the loveliest thing I have ever seen, small, slender, beautifully made with an entrancing smile and the most engaging, childlike simplicity of both manners and conversation.

Our last couple – for their passionate friendship warrants, and, indeed, calls for, that description – were two women named Billie Kennett and Elysée Barnes. One reported crime for a local paper, the other wrote up the latest fashions and even illustrated her work with her own charming sketches. She was also employed at times as a model and I think that she made a good deal of the money which kept them both. Billie, who was short, square and dark, a karate expert and a confirmed Women's Libber, adored her to what, for outsiders, was often an embarrassing degree, but which Elysée accepted with nonchalance and tacit approval, although, having once made a pass at Elysée myself, I have the impression that, when the right man comes along, she'll ditch Billie like a pair of torn tights.

All these people had apartments in the house, but Niobe had also converted the stables into a small bungalow which she had named The Lodge. This had been rented by a female recluse. Miss Minnie was, and remained, an enigma. She had opted for the bungalow, Niobe told me, as soon as she had seen the advertisement of it. She claimed that she edited the esoteric journal of a small religious sect called the Panconscious People, but had volunteered no other information about herself. However, Niobe claimed that, like Edmund Blunden's barn, Miss Minnie was old, not strange.

To mark my return home I had a house-warming party for which I gave word of mouth invitations, calling at each apartment as the simplest and most direct means of getting to know something about my tenants.

I chose a Sunday for my visits to them and set aside the following Sunday for the party. This was because some of the tenants were out and about on their lawful occasions during the week and in the evenings, but on Sundays, as Niobe had told me, all were to be found in residence.

Evesham and Constance gave me a drink, so did Polly and Cassie and the two girls, Billie and Elysée. Sumatra and Irelath refused the invitation, although charmingly. Sumatra said, 'Sunday is sacred to love-making, Chelion, so, although we are pleased to see you, please go away.' Irelath said, 'We're only young once, Chelion. Can't afford to let the golden days slip by. Obliged for the invitation all the same.'

Mandrake Shard thanked me for my invitation, which he accepted, but told me apologetically that he did not drink. 'Used to be an alcoholic. Daren't touch the stuff now, my dear fellow.' I promised we would lay on coffee. Coffee, of the instant variety, was also supplied to me by Latimer Targe when I called with my invitation. He said he had run out of whisky. He accepted the invitation and volunteered to 'bring a couple of bottles, old man, if you like, in case you run short. I know what these literary types can put away when the drinks are on the house'. I assured him that there would be no shortage, but I thanked him for the kind thought and decided that I did not like him very much after all.

Niobe had volunteered to help the cook manufacture the cocktail snacks, but I had vetoed this. 'Snacks for a dozen people, most of whom probably eat like wolves?' I said. 'It would take both of you all the week, and cook would probably give notice. No, my dear girl. I think we'll let a caterer cope,' I added firmly.

There remained Miss Minnie, the woman apart. I had felt enough curiosity about her to examine, in Niobe's office, her tenancy agreement. She had signed it Minnie, D-J (Miss). I took it that D-J were the initials of her baptismal names and was intrigued by the hyphen. I pointed it out to Niobe, who said, to my slight surpise:

'I don't believe Minnie is her real name. She is hiding from avaricious relatives, I expect.'

'Well, I hope she's not a criminal fleeing from justice,' I answered lightly.

She did not answer my repeated knocking on her door, so I thought, as it was a fine day, that she might be in the garden at the back of the house. You may have seen descriptions of my property in the newspapers, Dame Beatrice, but perhaps I had better give a short account of its situation and lay-out.

I have mentioned a seaside town and its shops, but actually we had the sea itself at the bottom of the front lawn, just beyond Miss M's bungalow. The gardens and park were at the back of the house, but in front there was this lawn which went down to the almost semi-circular inlet in a much larger bay on whose opposite shore the white-walled town, less than a mile away as the crow flies, could always be seen from our lawn unless the weather was misty. The deception lay in the fact that to reach the town by road involved a journey of ten miles along narrow twisting lanes (one could not call them roads) which made safe walking out of the question, apart from the added difficulty that the countryside was extremely hilly.

Our inlet was attractive enough at high tide, when the sea almost lapped against the grass verge, less so when the tide was low, for then we had an expanse of uninviting muddy sand between us and the sea. I used to bathe on the incoming tide, but I was (so far as I know) the only resident who ever went for a swim there. Knowing, as I suppose you do, what has happened, you will realise the importance of this and the part it has played in my predicament.

The town was on the south side of the big bay of which our inlet was so tiny a part, so my house faced north. It was entered from an ornate but not unpleasing portico which had been built on at a date much later than the building itself in order, I suppose, to add to the importance of the façade. Below a very high bank which formed one of the boundaries of the front lawn there were the stables (now converted to Miss Minnie's bungalow), which caused me to think that, before the portico had been added, the true front of the house had faced south, overlooking the gardens and park, for all the best rooms also faced that way. This proved important later on, for it meant that for the other tenants Miss Minnie's bungalow was out of sight.

(3)

This seems a long preamble, but Rufford has told me not to

leave anything out. So far as my house-warming party was concerned, I don't think there is anything to say. Miss Minnie was not in the garden and I hardly liked to snoop around her bungalow peering in at windows, so I concluded either that she was out or that she chose not to answer my knocking. I got Niobe to type an invitation to the house-warming and asked her to put it, in an envelope, through Miss Minnie's letterbox. A typed reply came next day, Miss Minnie would thank me not to interrupt her Sunday devotions by hammering on her door and was not interested in drunken orgies. I handed this missive to Niobe, who sniffed and filed it.

'Worth keeping, I think, the horrid old cat,' she said. At the party itself Mandrake Shard drank the strong coffee Niobe had prepared for him, backed into a corner to show her some tricks with a piece of string and left soon afterwards, afraid, I suppose, poor little devil, of being tempted to have a drink.

Billie and Elysée got a bit tight and then treated us to the quarrel scene in *Julius Caesar* between Brutus and Cassius which, I must admit, they did extremely well.

Polly Hempseed got drunk and offered to fight Evesham Evans for refusing to swap mates for the evening and night. Cassie McHaig boxed his ears and took him back to their apartment in disgrace.

Evesham Evans, who had handled the situation well, and Constance Kent, who had completely ignored it, proved to be ideal guests in that both remained sober. Latimer Targe got maudlin tipsy and insisted upon kissing Niobe and advising me to make an honest woman of her before it was too late. He stayed long after the others had gone and, in the end, I dragged him to his room and gave him a large whisky doped with aspirin and left him lying on his bed. He was contrite next day and begged my pardon for misbehaving himself with Niobe. He wanted to apologise to her, too, but I headed him off.

'What a shame!' said Niobe. 'He might have kissed me again!' We discussed Miss Minnie's unkind and unnecessary comments on what she had supposed our house-warming would be like.

'In a sense I suppose she wasn't so very far wrong,' I said, 'when you think of that young goat Hempseed and his wife-swapping nonsense and Targe going all maudlin and making scandalous suggestions to me about you.'

'Yes,' said Niobe a trifle frostily, I thought. (Could she have enjoyed the old reprobate's drunken kisses?) 'Yes, perhaps Miss Minnie wasn't so far wrong, as you say, but, you know, Chelion, I think Billie Kennett is right. She says nobody could be so secretive and peculiar as Miss Minnie unless she was a woman with a past.'

'I expect she's a reformed and retired Madame,' I said lightly. 'She has the look of one.'

'You get the idea from having spent a year in Paris, I suppose,' said Niobe, markedly changing her tone.

'Not at all. Just my imagination functioning. In France I don't believe a Madame ever retires.'

'Anyway, I'm glad Miss Minnie didn't come to the party. I wish Irelath and Sumatra hadn't turned it down, though. We could have done with them. The others were a pretty stodgy lot,' said Niobe, 'whether they got drunk or stayed sober.'

'Billie and Elysée,' I suggested, 'were lively enough.'

'They make me sick. You know, I still have old-fashioned prejudices, Chelion.'

'Live and let live is my motto. They won't do any harm if they're left alone,' I said uncomfortably.

'I suppose you'd say that about a tarantula or a black mamba!'

'Why not? – provided it didn't choose *me* for its victim, of course, and neither of the girls is likely to do that.'

I hoped she did not know of the rush I had so misguidedly given Elysée, so I changed the subject with what may have been injudicious haste when she said, with a certain emphasis, '*Neither* of the girls?'

'Why,' I asked, 'are you glad that Miss Minnie did not come to the party? Just because some of the company got tight and stepped a bit out of line? She may be a curmudgeonly old harridan, but it seems to me that she must be a pretty lonely one. Do her good to see something of the rest of us, one would have thought.'

'She sees something of Elysée Barnes,' said Niobe. 'That nymph picks her up in their little car when Billie Kennett isn't using it and runs her into the town for shopping.'

'How do you know?'

'Because I keep my eyes and ears open.'

'But I thought Miss Minnie had refused all offers of a lift into the town.'

'From the *men*, yes. Incidentally, what was in that letter you opened *by mistake* the other day?'

Well, now, Dame Beatrice, I had better come clean about that letter. It had lain on the hall table for a couple of days without being claimed and it had been postmarked with one of those advertising slogans the Post Office is so fond of. The result was that the name of the intended recipient was almost obscured. Thinking that I had better find out for whom it was intended, I slit the letter open, but as soon as I saw that it began: 'Dear Sister in Pan,' I guessed for whom it was intended and, as Niobe was about to walk into the village and would be passing near enough to the bungalow, I asked her to drop it in, and remarked that I would tell the postman that any correspondence for Miss Minnie should be left at The Lodge. I slipped a note in with the letter apologising for having opened it in error and suggesting that Miss Minnie make a point of informing her correspondents of her correct address.

'I have no idea what was in the letter,' I said, nettled by Niobe's tone. 'Have *you*? You took it over to her.'

'I do know something of what was in it, Chelion,' said Niobe, 'but not because I read it. Miss Minnie herself tackled me about it because the letter had been opened. She was furious about it. "I suppose that upstart thinks I have no claim," she said, "but this house is mine. He can open all the letters he likes, but one day I shall make my claim good and he can go back to his job as bath-attendant." '

I had no idea that Miss Minnie knew of my swimming pool era. I could only suppose that she had instituted some enquiries. I certainly thought she had a bee in her bonnet about my inheritance, so all I said was:

'If she can prove her claim, good luck to her. Does she think she ought to have Mrs Dupont-Jacobson's money as well?'

Naomi said, eyeing me without friendliness.

'I don't know. I only know that she begrudges the rent she pays. She told me so and gave me the reason. She claims that she was Mrs Dupont-Jacobson's next of kin and that a later will exists than the one which gave you the property.'

'You had better refer her to the lawyers. Heaven knows I don't want to do her out of her rights, if she has any, but I don't really think she has,' I said.

'Of course she hasn't. If you ask me, she's just a bewildered, rather nasty old thing with a grudge against you.'

I was not easy in my mind. It had never seemed to me likely that Mrs Dupont-Jacobson had no living relatives. There was every chance that one day (and sooner rather than later) one of them would turn up and contest the will, but the lawyers had been satisfied that everything was in order and I had taken their word for it. Now I began to doubt, as I had done at first, and my mind was not eased by a series of small, but, it seems to me now, significant events which followed my house-warming party.

(4)

The first of these was ludicrous, rather than alarming. At Niobe's instigation we had decided to re-name the house. So far, it had been called Creek Dupont.

'It's an awful name,' said Niobe. 'It sounds like a not too choosy country club with a dubious reputation.'

'Well, that's what you've turned it into, by and large,' I pointed out. 'Still, I'd like to get rid of the Dupont angle, ungrateful to my benefactor though it may be to say so. Anyway, what shall we call it?'

'We ought to connect it with the village, I suppose. We shall have to notify the Post Office if we change the name, but that should be a simple enough matter.'

'And the inmates must be told, so that they can notify their correspondents – and that includes Miss Minnie.'

'Yes, of course. How about presenting each flat with a packet of headed notepaper? Let's give them a little surprise. People are tickled to death to be given things free of charge.'

The nearest village was called Polweston. After some thought, we discarded the first syllable and settled for Weston Pipers. (Piper, of course, is my own surname and I was rather flattered when Niobe suggested that we use it.) We notified the Post Office of the change and ordered the notepaper.

Again at Niobe's suggestion, we had never numbered the apartments, as all letters came by way of the front door and it was my business – although actually, as her office opened off the hall, Niobe often made it hers – to put out the correspondence on a small table just to the left of the front door (to which all had keys) so that people could come and collect their letters at their convenience. The exception, of course, was Miss Minnie, whose correspondence, if any, was delivered through her own front door at The Lodge – or should have been, as I pointed out to Niobe.

The first news that there had been a printer's error of some magnitude came from Constance Kent. The printer's boy had delivered the packages by hand at midday on that particular morning. I had asked for the packets to be made up separately for each tenant, so when the boy arrived, as Niobe was on the telephone to one of our tradesmen, I set out the packages, each with a typed name on the cover, so that each tenant could pick up his or her own. I intended to put Miss Minnie's through her letter-box later, as hers was addressed like the rest and so did not include the words The Lodge, although I assumed she would add those two words herself to the headed notepaper.

I had notified the tenants that there was to be a change of address with the arrival, sooner or later, of complimentary packets of notepaper, and apparently Constance Kent, who, when she was not visiting her publishers or her literary agent or had some other reason for going up to London, was always in residence, had seen the boy's arrival. She was down the stairs and into the hall while I was still setting out the packages on the hall table.

'Ah!' she said, picking up the one with her name on it. 'You didn't say what the new address was to be. I should like to have seen proofs, but I suppose you didn't bother to ask for any. You amateurs!'

She tore off the wrappings and uttered an incredulous yelp. 'Oh, no! Oh, no!' she said; and burst into hysterical shrieks of laughter. 'Oh, how absolutely priceless! The printer's error to end *all* printers' errors, and God knows how we suffer from those!' She thrust the top sheet of her notepaper under my nose and I saw the heading. *Nest of Vipers* it said, in beautiful italic type.

CHAPTER 3

Departure of Miss Minnie

(1)

Of course the whole consignment had to go back to the printers. I took it to them myself, with the intention of giving them a piece of my mind and insisting upon a replacement free of charge and, needless to say, free of errors. To my astonishment they produced a typed sheet which justified and completely absolved them.

'Seems to me, Mr Piper,' said the manager, 'that one of your literary ladies or gents has been having a bit of a game with you. I'm afraid we'll have to charge you for the work. The mistake is none of our making, as you can see for yourself. Here's your order, sir, and here's your signature.'

'It's a forgery! That isn't my writing!'

'We were not to know that, sir, were we?'

I took the notepaper back with me to Weston Pipers. Since I had to pay for it, it belonged to me, anyway.

Niobe said: 'The address doesn't take up much space at the top of each sheet. The guillotine will soon chop it off and we'll keep all the notepaper for our own use, so it won't be a dead loss and anyway I forgot to remind you to ask for envelopes to match. I'll just type out the new address again and we'll have cards printed for the tenants to send to their friends.'

'I'll have another firm do the job, and it won't be a local one this time, I can tell you,' I said, remembering the manager's amusement.

'Nest of Vipers, eh?' he had chuckled. 'Oh, well, sir, let's hope the old saying won't work out in this case.'

'Old saying?'

'That there's many a true word spoken in jest, sir.'

Well, Constance Kent spread the story around and it became a tiresome joke for a bit. For my own satisfaction I put

out one or two feelers in order to pin down the joker, but with
no success. I put it squarely up to Billie Kennett and to Irelath
Moore, to whose sense of humour I thought the altered address
might well appeal, but both denied having perpetrated the
jape. Irelath said that he wished he *had* thought of it. Billie
said that she would have been delighted to have such an
address on her notepaper, but had not the wit to think of
anything so clever. I was forced to believe their denials and no
clue so far has turned up to explain the substituted address.

The next *contretemps* was received with mixed feelings among
our little group. It began with a conversation between Latimer
Targe and Elysée Barnes. Owing to the nature of her work,
that of a crime reporter for the county newspaper, Billie
Kennett was out of the house most days and, owing to the
nature of *hers,* Elysée spent some of the week in London
attending fashion shows or studying the creations in the big
London shops, and the rest of the week indoors sketching her
cribs from what she had seen, writing up her copy (a word, for
her, with a double meaning) and otherwise passing the time
until Billie came home.

This meant that she was quite often alone in the apartment
she shared with Billie and as, unlike Billie, she was a
gregarious young woman, she would invite one or other of us
to coffee or a drink or a stroll in the gardens with her. The two
girls owned a car (Niobe had arranged for half a dozen
well-screened lock-ups to be erected near the back of the
house), but Elysée, on her days at home, never drove it
because, on those occasions, Billie used it to get to her
newspaper office. When Elysée had to go up to Town, she
drove to the nearest station, nearly ten miles away, and left the
car there against her return, while Billie took herself to work
on her moped. It was on these occasions, I suppose, that Elysée
dropped Miss Minnie in the town.

Because in some respects their occupations were complemen-
tary, Billie's as a crime reporter, Latimer's as a re-hasher of
past crimes, he was the only male friend of Elysée's upon
whom Billie did not look with a jealous and jaundiced eye. His
work entailed a great deal of research, so he was often out of
the house, but when he was at home he and Elysée were
usually in one another's company. I suppose she showed him

her sketches and he, no doubt, regaled her with an account of his often gruesome discoveries. Anyway, they liked to be together, although Elysée never pushed her luck to the extent of neglecting Billie in favour of Latimer Targe, neither do I think he would have wanted her to do so.

'I've stayed out of woman trouble ever since my wife died, old boy,' he said to me when we were having a drink together one evening. 'It's not that I don't like women, but once bitten twice shy, and one thing about these two girls, they're *safe*, if you know what I mean. You can *talk* to them and that's where it begins and ends.' (As I have stated, I did not think this need be true in Elysée's case, but I was not prepared to argue.)

I am sorry if this seems to be a digression, Dame Beatrice, but I think perhaps what follows will explain it. I know that the impudent joke about the name of the house and this friendship between Targe and Elysée seem unimportant, and I suppose they *would* have been unimportant except for what happened next.

The first inkling I had that the jest was not as innocent as I had supposed came from Latimer Targe himself. As I have mentioned, he made a living by re-hashing true stories of murder. He was, I would have thought, far too hardboiled a type to busy himself with the occult. The thing did not begin in that way, however. He joined me as I was strolling beside the lake in the grounds one morning and his silence gave me the impression that he had something on his mind. We paced along side by side for a bit and then he unburdened himself.

'I say, old man, I've been looking up the records,' he said. 'I mean the records of this place, you know, this nest of vipers.'

'Oh, look here,' I said, 'surely that joke has grown whiskers by now!'

'Sorry, old man. Didn't mean to rib you. There was murder done here, you know. I looked it all up in the county library. Year of 1786. Owner got one of the maids into trouble and when her father – one of the tenants – came up to make a fuss about it, the squire shot him dead.'

'So what happened?' I asked. 'Even in 1786 landowners couldn't murder their tenants with impunity.'

'Oh, the squire got off. His bailiff swore that the farmer, or

whatever he was, had come armed with a dirty great knife and
that the shooting had been done in self-defence.'

'And the court accepted that?'

'They did. The person who got hanged was the girl. She lay
in wait for the squire, persuaded him to dismount from his
horse, enticed him into the cottage she had shared with her
father and as she followed him into the bedroom she hit him
over the head with an axe.'

'Couldn't *she* have pleaded self-defence?'

'Well, that's the story as I unearthed it, old boy, but mark
the sequel, as they say. This house is haunted.'

'By the murdered eighteenth-century owner?'

'Don't laugh, old boy. No, by the killer herself. Been seen
about the rooms looking for the squire all over again.'

'Your readers are not likely to swallow that one. I thought
your stories were strictly factual,' I said.

'I suppose a ghost is a fact like any other. Anyway, don't you
be so sceptical. The woman's been seen, I tell you.'

'Ah, and, as the priest said to the man who confessed to
murder, how many times?'

'Three in all.' He repeated it. 'Three times in all.'

'By whom?' I dropped my jocose attitude. A house like mine
might well offer a temptation to burglars.

'Twice by those two girls – they share a bedroom, you
know – and once by your partner.'

'By Niobe? Nonsense! She would have told me.'

'She thought she'd been dreaming until she got together
with Miss Barnes and they swapped stories,' said Targe. 'It was
Miss B. who told me all about it. I advised her to complain. I
was joking, of course, but then Niobe agreed she'd seen it, too.'

I tackled Niobe forthwith. She was in what had been the
housekeeper's dayroom. She had furnished it at small expense
but with taste and had retained its cupboards with their
ornate, beautifully-wrought brass handles which she saw to it
were kept equally beautifully polished by the char who 'did'
for most of the tenants, according them a day or a halfday a
week, as their wishes and, I suppose, their incomes dictated.
She was what people who employ charwomen call a superior
type, came in her own mini and charged the earth, but she was
a splendidly conscientious worker and I am sure earned her

princely pay. Anyway, in our out of the way spot, I was glad to get anybody so good and those tenants who queried her prices were soon told to take her services or leave them, and that was that. She and Niobe, for some reason, got on particularly well together.

'Look here, Niobe,' I said, as soon as Mrs Smith's mini was churning up the gravel on its departure, 'what's this story about the ghost of a murderess?'

'It isn't a ghost,' she said, 'and I think you had better have anti-burglar devices put on all the downstair windows because that's the way she is managing to get inside this place, I'm sure.'

'She?' (But, of course, there was only one person she could mean.)

'Miss Minnie. She's got this bee in her bonnet about a will of a later date than the one which made the property over to you. I think she's begun creeping about trying to find it. You would do well to get rid of her, Chelion. I don't think she's right in the head.'

'It's up to you to get rid of her,' I said. 'You were the person who let her have The Lodge.'

'It's your property, not mine. *I* can't turn her out.'

I had special fastenings put on all the downstair windows and we left it at that. I did not feel prepared to tackle Miss Minnie myself.

(2)

As, I suppose, might have been expected, the next item was a flood of anonymous letters, most of them addressed either to Niobe or to me. They accused us of 'living in sin'.

'Miss Minnie again, of course,' said Niobe. 'She really will have to go.'

'On what excuse? She has signed for a three-year tenancy, and we have no evidence to prove that she writes – or, rather, types – the letters,' I pointed out. 'Hers is not the only typewriter in the place. Everybody has one except Targe. He sends his stuff out to be typed.'

'Or, of course, you could marry me and put an end to her nonsense. Where is that note Miss Minnie sent you to tell you

not to disturb her on the Sabbath?' Niobe had spoken the first
sentence lightly. On the next she had struck a serious note.

'I turned it over to you. Don't you remember?' I asked.

'Then it's been filed. Come along to my office. All type-
writers have their idiosyncrasies, so we shall soon know
whether her note was done on the same machine as these filthy
letters.'

'I wonder whether anybody else has had one?' I said.

'You or I would know, wouldn't we? One of us puts out the
letters on the hall table every day.'

'Oh, beyond just setting them out, I never bother to look at
them,' I said. 'I never even trouble to see whether more than one
is addressed to the same person. I don't make piles. I just lay
them out face upward and leave people to pick out their own.'

'Yes, you always were as lazy as Hall's dog, whoever *he* was,'
she said. 'Even at the swimming pool you left most of the work
to me. Still, you did pick up *one* letter which was not meant for
you.'

I had noted that she kept her office locked when she was not
in it. She unlocked it and we went through the files. Miss
Minnie's curt note was not there.

'Well, I must have filed it if you gave it me,' said Niobe. 'It
proves what I said. She is our ghost all right. When she
decided to send the anonymous letters she must have got into
this room and removed the only bit of her typing we had.'

'I don't see how she could have got in here if you always
keep this room locked,' I said.

'The windows, idiot! That's why I told you to get them
properly fastened at night.'

'By the way,' I said, as we went out, 'it isn't really Hall's dog
you meant; it was Ludlam's dog.'

'Oh, yes? And who was Ludlam?'

'According to the Reverend E. Cobham Brewer, L.L.D.,
who states that he got the story from Ray's *Proverbs,* Ludlam
was a famous Surrey witch who lived in a cave near Farnham.
Her dog was so lazy that it even rested its head against the
wall to bark.'

'My home was in Surrey,' said Niobe, laughing. 'But,' she
added, sobering down, 'what are we to do about these letters?'

'So far as you and I are concerned, I don't propose to give in to anonymous rubbish,' I said, laughing in my turn. 'But we'd better find out whether the letters are a nuisance to any of the others, or whether you and I are especially favoured.'

We soon knew the answer to that one. Billie came to me and said that she and Elysee would be giving up their tenancy. I referred her to Niobe, who pointed out that they had signed a three-year lease.

'Although actually,' Niobe said to me privately, 'I think we ought to let them go. They're rather an embarrassing couple, aren't they?'

'I don't find them so. Very nice girls. As for their little idiosyncrasy, well, there are plenty of others like them, especially in these days, as people are beginning to find out.'

'Personally I haven't much use for Women's Lib, and a misogynist like you wouldn't give a hoot *how* offensive to others their conduct is, so long as neither of them makes a pass at *you*,' said Niobe bitterly.

'But their conduct isn't offensive. They're most discreet,' I said. 'As for Elysée, I get the impression that, if the right chap came along, she would ditch Billie like a pair of laddered tights.' (I was rather proud of this simile, as you will have noticed.)

'I don't believe it! I'll tell them they can go, then, shall I?' Niobe asked.

'Did they mention any letters?' (I suppose the conclusion I jumped to was the obvious one.)

'No, only the ghost, but it's really the letters, I'm sure. They're bound to have had at least one. After all, they're pretty vulnerable, aren't they?'

'What, in these days? Still, if they want to leave, that's that.'

So the two quietest and best-behaved (so far as I was concerned) of our tenants took their leave of us, and their modest apartment on the second floor remained empty. What is more, the anonymous letters ceased as soon as Billie and Elysée had gone.

'So we were wrong in suspecting Miss Minnie, it seems,' said Niobe. 'It was those two little misfits who wrote them.'

'I don't believe it,' I said, 'You yourself thought that some of the letters came to them as well as to us, and that was the reason for their leaving.'

'Oh, anonymous letter-writers always include themselves. I thought everybody knew that.'

'Maybe, but people who live in glass houses don't throw stones at their own dwellings. There's still plenty of prejudice against emotional friendships between women.'

'Only the other day you denied all that. What a turncoat you are. What with the witch's dog and an altered proverb, I really *am* learning things this week!' said Niobe.

(3)

You must not think, Dame Beatrice, that this account covers only a few days. There were quite long gaps between one happening and the next, and I suppose more than six weeks elapsed between the episode of the notepaper heading and the departure of Miss Kennett and Miss Barnes.

Niobe had asked them to let her have their new address so that she could send on any letters which came for them, but I suppose they had already notified the Post Office, for none of their correspondence turned up, and neither did they leave a forwarding address.

The next couple to go were Sumatra and Irelath, but although they departed from Weston Pipers at the end of September, they paid six months' rent in advance, asked for their apartment to be dusted and aired periodically, and promised to return in the following March. Irelath was to lecture in the United States and Sumatra resigned from her job in order to accompany him. I could only suppose that his Canadian father's money was grafting the trip, for Irelath was so very minor a poet, so far as his published work was concerned, that it was impossible to believe that he had been selected on his merits.

My novel matured slowly. As I finished each chapter Niobe typed it for me. She had invested in a new typewriter for the purpose because, she said, it was unsuitable that deathless prose such as mine should be typed on a ten-year-old machine. That would do for making out receipts to the tenants for their rent and lists for the tradespeople, but not for my novel. Whether she was serious in her stated admiration for my work, or whether she simply wanted a new toy to play with, I did not enquire. I subbed up for the typewriter and I must say that she made my chapters look very attractive indeed, so much so that I began to admire them myself and felt that, given beginner's luck, publication ceased to be problematical and was a near-certainty.

So matters went on for a month or two. The sea became colder, my swims from our strip of beach less frequent, the tenants, as the soldier said of the camp-following prostitutes, became more and more like old war-comrades and we all settled down to winter in. The house was snug and comfortable, for Niobe had installed a splendid central-heating system and had provided electric fires as well. The tenants' excursions up to town to harry their publishers and abuse their literary agents became as infrequent as my dips in the sea and, except for some unexplained excursions into the town, everybody stayed put, although harmony did not always prevail. I was aware of undercurrents.

My novel reached the halfway stage and sometimes I wondered why on earth I had ever begun it. At about this time – I can't remember the exact date – the weather turned wet and Constance Kent hit Evesham Evans over the head with a bottle with (according to his account) no justification whatever. He had to have four stitches in the cut. Polly Hempseed and Cassie McHaig got roaring drunk on the latter's birthday and went staggering out into the grounds naked as they were born and performed weird gyrations on the lawn while the rain poured down on them and Niobe sent me out to remonstrate with them while everybody else crowded the windows to watch. Latimer Targe followed me out with a couple of blankets. We threw these over them to cover their nakedness although, as he said regretfully afterwards, it did rather spoil the fun for everybody, and when we got them indoors they had a fight which wrecked their living-room.

One morning when the postman knocked me up and presented me with a registered letter for which a signature was required, I signed obediently, having no idea, until he had gone and I had taken it to my room and a better light, that the letter was not for me but was addressed to Miss Minnie at The Lodge.

'Oh, damn!' I thought, as I looked out at the pouring rain,

the soaked lawn and the dripping November trees. 'She'll have to wait for it. I'm not trapesing out in this!'

However, a registered letter is a registered letter, so, cursing the weather and ignoring Niobe's call that breakfast was ready, I put a waterproof over my pyjamas, put on some shoes and ran across the lawn. Lights were on in several parts of the house, but the bungalow was unlighted and the curtains, I could see, were still drawn. I pushed the registered envelope through the letter-box, beat an exasperated tattoo on the door and pelted back to the house to get dried and dressed.

Niobe was not very pleased.

'No need to have gone out there before breakfast,' she said. 'I've kept yours hot, but it isn't the same as when it's first cooked. She'll probably stay in bed till eleven or later, on a beastly dark morning like this.'

'Not with the bashing I gave her front door,' I said.

'I wonder what was in the envelope? Did you open it as you opened the other one?' Niobe asked nastily.

'Money, perhaps, as it was registered,' I said, ignoring the thrust.

I thought no more of the matter. We were already making preparations for Christmas and I had planned a cocktail party, with a Christmas tree and presents for everybody. On Christmas Eve, Hempseed and Cassie, unusually subdued and well-behaved since their Terpsichorean exhibition on the lawn, could be heard in their flat practising carols to Constance Kent's guitar, while the sounds of sawing and hammering from the Evans-Kent apartment seemed to prove that Evesham was carrying out a promise he had made to Cassie, a devout Catholic whenever she troubled herself to go to church – hers was a long way off – that he would make her a crib.

All seemed set for a happy if not a particularly peaceful period when the postman came again with an offering for Miss Minnie. This time it was a fairly bulky parcel.

'This is the third time I've brought it, and never nobody at home,' he told me resentfully, 'and in this weather, sir, that's not funny. There is never nobody at home in that bungalow, not to take in that registered letter nor nothing, so, without you're willing to take it in for the lady, I'll have to leave her a note that she'll have to go and collect this parcel herself from the Post Office. I've done more than my duty already and I can't tote this here parcel around no more times. It would mean her going into the town for it if I don't leave it with you. Please yourself, of course, sir. You don't have to accept it if you don't want.'

'Oh, I'll take it,' I said. I put it down underneath the hall table, did not think to tell anyone else that I had taken it in and, in the general bustle of preparations, Christmas shopping, ordering in drinks and food and being driven almost demented by Constance Kent's guitar and Evesham Evans's incessant carpentry, I forgot all about it. It was not until our expensive and cultured charwoman complained about it that it came to my mind that it had been in my possession for some days.

'Which, if I have moved that parcel once, sir, in order to clean the hall floor, I have moved it twenty times,' she said angrily.

This I knew to be picturesque exaggeration, but she had made her point.

'Good Lord! I'd forgotten it was there,' I said. I fished it out and went out in the rain to deliver it. I failed in my object. The curtains of the bungalow were still drawn and seemed to say, like Macbeth's porter, 'Knock, knock, knock! Who's there, i' the other devil's name? ... But this place is too cold for hell.'

I continued to knock. Then I began to shout. Then I banged on each of the bungalow windows in turn. Then I became alarmed. Poor old Miss Minnie, I concluded, had been taken ill. We were so used never to see her about that it had not occurred to me to wonder why she had not answered the door to the postman or made any enquiries about a parcel which, ten to one, she must have been expecting. I felt bad about the parcel. It probably contained a Christmas present.

I tore back to the house and hammered on Evans's and then on Targe's door. It would not take the three of us to break the kitchen window, which was the only one uncurtained, but I did not want the responsibility of being alone in discovering Miss Minnie either desperately ill or even dead in bed.

She was dead all right, and she was in bed. There had been water everywhere and her head was in the most dreadful mess.

It was Latimer Targe who dealt competently with the situation. He was hardboiled mentally, no doubt, by his years of researching into violent crime. He sprinted back to the house and telephoned for a doctor and the police after telling Evesham and me to remain in the bungalow until the authorities took over.

'Surely there is no need for *both* of us to stay here,' said Evesham, who had turned white and looked as though he might be sick at any moment.

'Oh, yes, there is,' said Targe. 'You are each other's witness that nothing is altered or disturbed before the police get here. This ruddy woman has got herself murdered.'

There was not a trace of pity for poor old Miss Minnie in his tone. I wondered whether he knew more about the dead woman that I did.

CHAPTER 4

Routine Enquiries

(1)

As you have asked me to go on with my account, Dame Beatrice, I will write it as though you have not seen the newspapers or talked with my solicitor.

I suggested to Evans that, so long as we stuck together, there was no reason why we had to stay in the room with the dead woman. He seemed glad to agree to this, so we repaired to Miss Minnie's little sitting-room.

Like all the sitting-rooms up at the house, that at the bungalow was furnished with an electric fire and had no open fireplace. It was a little surprising, therefore, to see a heavy old-fashioned brass poker lying on the hearthrug. Evans picked it up.

'Wonder what she wanted with this?' he said, swinging it to and fro.

'Brought it with her from her old home, thinking there would be coal fires here, I expect,' I said. 'By the way, ought you to have handled it? Targe rather warned us, I thought, that nothing ought to be touched.'

'Oh, he meant in the bedroom, of course,' he said. He began to hum in a tuneless sort of way and continued to swing the poker. 'I say, you do realise somebody must have murdered the old girl, don't you? I mean, Targe was right.'

'She may have drowned herself, but she hardly bashed her own face in,' I said, 'and for God's sake stop swinging that poker about!' My voice cracked. I could not control it.

'Sorry,' he said. 'Nerves.'

'Well, put it down, man.'

But, although he stopped swinging it about, he retained his hold on it. I can see his reason now, of course. At the time I thought he was in the same upset state as I was and that the

feel of the poker gave him confidence. I see now that he
suspected me all along and was holding on to the poker as a
means of defence in case I set about him and made my escape
before the police turned up, and I see that his desire to return
to the house was not to get away from the corpse but to get
away from *me!* At the time, however, such a thought was far
from my mind. I pulled myself together and tried to do some
logical thinking, for the police would arrive at any moment
and would be asking questions, no doubt, of all of us, but of
me in particular as the owner of the bungalow and especially
as the person who had summoned assistance in order to break
into it. No use telling them I had no key to it, so far as I knew.

But, so far as I could see, there was no logic about the
matter. So far as the rest of us were concerned, Miss Minnie
had hardly existed. It was true that she had been a social
misfit, an oddity, a recluse, a misplaced person in our little
community. It was also true that she had claimed to be Mrs
Dupont-Jacobson's rightful heiress, and it was possible that
she was a snooper, a pseudo-ghost and the probable writer of
anonymous letters. It was obvious that she objected to
innocent merrymaking, but, allowing for all this, I could see
no reason for anybody's having gone to the extreme length of
murdering her.

I recalled the joke – it could have been nothing more –
made by Billie Kennett that Miss Minnie must be a woman
with a past and I remembered my own facetious observation
and began to wonder whether the printer had been right and
that indeed a true word had been spoken in jest and also that
something or someone connected with Miss Minnie's past had
at last caught up with her.

On the other hand there were those anonymous letters. That
they were libellous there was little doubt, but had one of them
contained a dangerous amount of truth, I wondered? I looked
at the brass poker dangling from Evesham Evans's powerful,
hairy fingers. I recalled the tough, he-man novels he wrote; his
noisy, violent quarrels with his wife; the fact that I knew
nothing of his background (although that was true of all of my
tenants, now I had come to think of it); nor did I know
whether he had received one of the letters.

My thoughts turned to little Mandrake Shard with his spy

stories full of violence, torture, double-crossings, and his self-confessed history of alcoholism. I thought of Latimer Targe, steeped in stories of real-life violent crime and of Billie Kennett who reported it. Whoever had played that joke and sent the printers that notepaper-heading may have guessed more truly than he knew when he called my house Nest of Vipers.

My random thoughts, having taken this direction, became canalised. I eyed the poker again. It could have been the agent with which Miss M's head had been battered. If so, and if he had done his homework, the murderer would have cleansed it of blood, hair and his own fingerprints before replacing it in the sitting-room.

Then, my shocked mind beginning to work overtime, I returned to wondering whether Evans was the murderer and, if so, whether perhaps he was deliberately re-imposing his fingerprints on the poker, holding me as witness that his prints were innocent ones.

'Two can play at that game,' I thought confusedly. You will understand, Dame Beatrice, that I was not myself at the time, or I would never have given way to such morbid imaginings. I spoke to him. 'Damn cold in here,' I said. 'Why don't we have the fire on?' I stooped and pressed the switch. 'Now *I* have some explicable fingerprints,' I thought.

'That's better,' he said. 'Ought to have thought of it for myself.'

'And so have put your seemingly innocent dabs on to something else you may have touched when you were here before,' I thought; and such was my disordered state that I only just stopped myself saying it aloud.

I suppose we must have sat there for the best part of an hour before anybody turned up. I don't know what Evans's thoughts were, but I know now that we were both adding two and two together and totalling them into a conclusion that the other fellow was a murderer. Looking back, I can see that if my mind had not been temporarily disturbed I would never have dreamed of suspecting Evans, but under the influence of shock one seldom thinks clearly.

The first person to turn up was the local doctor. He was accompanied by Targe. Evans and I went together to the front door – Evans first putting down the poker – to let them in, but Targe did not cross the threshold.

'So where is the body?' asked the doctor, coming in in a business-like way. 'Are you sure it is defunct?'

'Yes, nobody, not even you, can do her any good,' replied Evans in a phrase I suppose he had used to dramatic effect in one of his books. We took the doctor into the bedroom. He looked at the body on the bed.

'Well, well! What's all this?' he said. 'All right, you two need not stay. I can manage.'

'We are witnesses,' said Evans, 'to a very nasty business. We leave nobody alone here until the police arrive.'

The doctor shrugged his shoulders, took off his overcoat, turned up his cuffs and began, I suppose, a preliminary examination of the body. He had finished and was washing his hands in the bathroom (to which Evans and I had followed him, although I saw no point whatever in doing so, but Evans had caught my sleeve and steered me along) when the police turned up.

They sent us over to the house and then I suppose they went through the usual routine of photographs, fingerprints, agreement or otherwise between the doctor Targe had summoned and the police surgeon, and then, of course, they came over to the house and began the inevitable questioning of myself and the others. As Miss Minnie's landlord and one of the three who had found the body, I was interrogated first.

How long had I owned Weston Pipers?

For about two years and a half.

How long had the deceased been a tenant?

Ever since the alterations to the mansion had been completed.

How long ago was that?

Last May twelvemonth.

Why had the deceased rented the bungalow instead of taking an apartment in the house?

She was a recluse.

Could she have had an apartment instead of the bungalow if she had asked for one?

Yes, she could have had the choice of two, but she opted for the bungalow and would not consider anything else. My – I boggled a bit here, not knowing quite how to describe Niobe's position in my scheme of things – my housekeeper, who had been responsible for all the lettings while I was in Paris, would confirm.

Had I any previous acquaintance with the deceased before she rented the bungalow?

I certainly had not.

How did the deceased get on with the other tenants?

So far as I knew, she had had nothing to do with them at all.

Thank you, sir, that would be all for the moment. Would I ask my housekeeper to spare them a few minutes? Oh, by the way, sir, they noticed that I had fitted anti-burglar devices to my downstair windows. Had I had any particular reason for doing that?

No, it had been a precautionary measure, that was all.

Yet the same precautions, they had noticed, had not been extended to the bungalow.

No, they had not.

Why not, sir? Surely it was more necessary for the bungalow of an old lady living alone to be so protected, rather than a house which (they consulted a list) contained five able-bodied men?

Well, we – that is, my housekeeper – suspected that Miss Minnie herself broke into the house at night, so there was no point in fortifying the bungalow.

Why would Miss Minnie break in?

She seemed to have some idea that there was a will somewhere in the house which made her Mrs Dupont-Jacobson's heir and not myself.

Would I explain that, please.

So, of course, Dame Beatrice, I gave them the low-down on the whole business of how I had come by my inheritance and they made plenty out of it. It turned out that they had made enquiries and that the lawyers knew of no other will except the one which named me as the heir, but there was no doubt that Miss Minnie had been distantly related to my benefactress and the police did their best to make me admit that I had known this. I side-stepped them – quite truthfully – so then they began asking about the discovery of the body.

Why had I thought it necessary to have two witnesses with me when I broke into the bungalow?

Because I did not know whether Miss Minnie was ill or whether she was dead.

Why should I suppose she might be dead?

I didn't really suppose it.

So if I thought she might have been taken ill, wouldn't it have been more natural to have taken a woman – my housekeeper, for example – with me, rather than two men?

I discovered that we should have to break a window and climb in and men are better at that sort of thing than women.

Was there no spare key to the bungalow?

I had no idea. The tenants were supplied with keys to their rooms, although no longer to the front door of the house. We assumed there was always somebody about to let people in and my housekeeper was nervous about front door keys which might get lost, so we had collected them and locked them away. At this they returned to my breaking the window.

Had I no key to the bungalow?

Not that I knew of.

Miss Nutley was almost sure she had given me a spare key.

Well, of course, Dame Beatrice, all that was only the beginning of it. All the others were interrogated, but, according to the accounts they gave me of the interviews (at a mass meeting which Targe, who ghoulishly appeared to be in his element at the prospect of being mixed up in one of the real-life crimes which furnished him with the material for his books, insisted upon calling and which took place in my sitting-room), nobody could tell the police anything of importance.

We were all on tenterhooks for the next few days. An inquest was held and a verdict brought in of murder by person or persons unknown. Miss Minnie (identified by a smooth-faced, soft-voiced gentleman who announced himself as the proprietor of the quasi-religious journal of which Miss Minnie was editor) was buried at the journal's expense against the ultimate winding-up of her estate, floral tributes were sent by everybody in the house and, as the police made no reappearance at Weston Pipers for just over a fortnight, the reporters gave up pestering us and we went on much as usual.

If this seems a heartless and ill-conceived proceeding under the circumstances, it must be remembered that none of us had ever really known Miss Minnie and that, in any case, she had dissociated herself entirely from any of our activities. Soon, however, we were in the thick of the police enquiry once more.

It came as a surprise to all of us, I think. It certainly came as a shock to me. I suppose when all one asks for is a quiet life with no major upheavals, one is easily lured (as they say) into a false sense of security, so when Mrs Smith, who had been 'doing the hall' when they knocked, came to my sitting-room to tell me of their arrival, I felt the sense of panic I used to experience at school when an interview with the headmaster was pending.

'Well, show them in here,' I said.

'Which I have told them to wipe their boots before doing so, sir, the drive being that mucky you would not credit.'

'They can't have walked up the drive. They come in cars,' I said.

'Which they have walked over to The Lodge and back, as I have seen with my own eyes out of the hall windows, being as how I was polishing the table for the letters when I heard the car drive up.'

The Detective Chief Superintendent was affability itself.

'Sorry to trouble you again, sir, but there are one or two little matters.'

I invited him and his sergeant to sit down and offered them drinks.

'Not just at the moment, thank you, sir. We won't keep you long, but we think you may be able to help us to clear up a point or so.'

'Glad to do anything I can, of course,' I said; but I was far from happy. His manner was much too smooth.

'Thank you, sir. When you first saw the body, did you notice anything unusual about it?'

'I thought it was altogether unusual, Chief Superintendent. The last thing one expects to find on one's property is a dead body, let alone one with—with—' I had a sickening recollection of Miss Minnie's smashed-up face. At the inquest the medical evidence had given drowning as the cause of death, so the head injuries inflicted after death could only have been the act of a sadistic lunatic, I felt, and I was still trying to fight a queasy feeling in my stomach when he spoke again.

'There was something *on* the body, sir, which I thought you might have noticed.'

'I noticed as little as I could,' I said. 'One glance was enough for me. I had a job not to be sick.'

'Strange you did not notice this, sir. The other gentlemen, Mr Targe and Mr Evans, both noticed it and mentioned it to me before I even asked them about it.' He took an envelope from his pocket, opened it and drew out a bit of seaweed. It was a piece of the dark red, rather pretty, fernlike kind. Most of our local seaweed was either that brilliant green mossy-looking sort which grows on flat rocks which are covered at high tide, or else the glutinous long strands with little dark-brown bladders on them – horrible, slimy stuff, I always thought it. I had seen a few bits of the kind he showed me, but it was not all that common in our bay.

'Well, I may have seen it unconsciously,' I said, 'but I was too horrified to notice any details that I can remember.'

'I see, sir. I believe you were the manager of a swimming pool before you went over to Paris.'

'That's right, yes.'

'You must have been pleased when you found you had a natural bathing-place at the bottom of your lawn.'

'Yes, of course, but one hardly uses it at this time of year.'

'Not even an experienced swimmer such as yourself?'

'I'm not keen enough to want to catch pneumonia.'

His questions, no doubt, would have alarmed a guilty man even more than they alarmed me, but they made me very uneasy.

'Do you *never* go swimming in the winter, sir?'

'Yes, in an indoor swimming pool where they warm the water, and there is nothing of the sort in these parts.'

'But you never swim in the open sea?'

'Not in the winter, no.'

'You attended the inquest on the body?'

'Of course. Besides, I was one of the witnesses.'

'Quite so. There was one item of information which we asked the coroner not to mention. You will recollect that the medical evidence was of death by drowning.'

'Well?'

'Well, sir, haven't you something you would like to tell me about that?'

'There is nothing I can tell you about it. We thought she had attempted to drown herself, thought better of it, got as far as her bed and then collapsed.'

'And the state of her head, sir? How do you account for that?'

'I don't have to account for it. I suppose a burglar broke in and hit her in case she wasn't quite dead. It doesn't sound likely, but it's the only conclusion we could reach.'

'You used to swim in your little cove in the summer, of course?'

'Oh, yes, frequently, but the water was warm in the summer.'

'Did any of your tenants do the same?'

'They may have done. The bathing here is free. I don't keep track of everything my tenants do.'

'Did you ever know Miss Minnie to do anything of the sort? – to go bathing in the sea?'

'I knew almost nothing about her. In any case, the answer to that is the same as I have given you in connection with the other tenants. I had neither the time nor the inclination to keep tabs on their activities.'

'Your housekeeper has mentioned some obnoxious letters which came for you.'

'Not only for me. She herself had a couple and so did two of my tenants, two girls. There may have been others.'

'Two girls? Who would they be, sir?'

'A Miss Kennett and a Miss Barnes. They moved out a few weeks ago. I think the letters were the cause of their leaving.'

'Can you give me their present address, sir?'

'Sorry, but no. They didn't tell us where they were going to live. No doubt the Post Office would have an address for forwarding letters.'

'No doubt, sir. About the window-fastenings: you said, I think, that they were only a precautionary measure.'

'That's right.'

'But not entirely true, sir. I understood that you suspected the deceased of breaking into the house at night and prowling about in the other tenants' rooms.'

'I think that was other people's idea, not mine. I saw nobody prowling around, but I had the fastenings put on as a precautionary measure, just as I said.'

'Quite so, sir. You will forgive a very personal question, I hope? How did you come into possession of this property and the money to repair and convert it?'

'I told you that, the last time you were here. I was left the money and the estate by a Mrs Dupont-Jacobson who entertained the remarkable theory that I had saved her from drowning.'

'In the sea, sir?'

'Yes, off Funchal, Madeira.'

'We know that the deceased claimed to be Mrs Dupont-Jacobson's next of kin. Are you sure she proposed to contest the will?'

'So I was informed. I was never approached personally in the matter.'

'But you were sufficiently impressed by what you had heard to go to your solicitors about it.'

'Merely another precautionary measure, Chief Superintendent. I was assured that there was no substance in the claim.'

'That must have gratified you, sir.'

'Not particularly. If the claim had been a valid one, the time to have made it was when the will was proved, not more than two years afterwards.'

'Two years, sir?'

'More than. Nearer three. I was a year in Paris while the renovations and some structural alterations were carried out, and my tenants, as I told you, have been in residence since May twelvemonth.'

'Thank you for your help, sir. I wonder whether you can place a room at the disposal of my sergeant and myself?'

'Do you mean you want an interview room? I thought you saw everybody on your first visit.'

'Mr Evans and Mr Targe, who were with you when you broke into the bungalow, may be able to help us.'

'Well, I expect my housekeeper will be prepared to give up her office to you for an hour or so.'

He and the sergeant remained for the rest of the morning. When they had gone, little Shard came to see me. The tenants wanted another mass meeting. Evans was to take the chair and they hoped very much that Niobe and I would be present.

This sounded ominous. Niobe thought so, too. She said she did not like it. They must have been putting their heads together. She hoped that the mass meeting was not to herald a mass walk-out.

'Well, I suppose you couldn't blame them,' I said. 'Nobody likes being mixed up with the police, especially in a case of murder.'

The mass meeting took place in Evans's large sitting-room immediately after lunch and Niobe's pious hopes were soon dashed. It was clear that, as soon as the police would allow it, a mass walk-out was planned.

Evans, as one would expect, proved a competent, business-like chairman. He was hospitable, too. Coffee and an assortment of liqueurs were dispensed by Constance. The armchairs, some indigenous, some borrowed, were extremely comfortable. The tenants settled down ghoulishly.

'I want to make it clear,' said Evans, 'that no personal feelings are involved. I'm sure we have all been very happy at Weston Pipers and the last thing we would have wanted is to leave.'

Here Niobe spoke up with some abruptness.

'I hope you remember that you have all signed a three-year agreement,' she said.

'So had Billie and Elysée,' Constance Kent pointed out, 'but they went and so shall we.'

'Please! No arguments at this stage,' said her husband, 'although circumstances do alter cases. The point is, Chelion, that whereas the fact of a murder wouldn't do some of us any harm because of the nature of our work, it must have its effect on others of us. Besides, all this police questioning and probing is a confounded waste of our time and it also saps our concentration. I need all my energies for a damned Chapter Eight which is refusing to come right. I am not willing to expend them answering questions from the Chief Superintendent about matters which are no concern of mine.'

'But you would still be subject to questioning, even if you left today,' said Niobe.

'Granted, and I have no doubt I could survive it, but there are others, as I say.'

'Including me,' said the soldierly Constance. 'The publicity over this business will be the ruin of my books. You can write pulsating stories of star-crossed lovers, or you can get yourself mixed up in a sordid case of the murder of a defenceless, grey-haired old woman, but you can't do both.'

'Oh, there I think you exaggerate, Constance,' said Targe.

'No, I don't. Maybe your own work won't suffer at all. You may even be able to make capital out of this awful business, as will Mandrake and even Cassie.'

'Don't you believe it,' said Cassie McHaig. 'My paper is very finicky about its reporters getting mixed up with the police. I'm supposed to champion the cause of the downtrodden, not to get myself a bit of notoriety by being questioned about the brutal murder of an old lady.'

'Before we go any further,' said Targe, 'there is something I think Chelion ought to know. I've told the others, Chelion, and, to put our cards on the table, it is the real reason for our wanting to leave.'

'I'm not sure this is the time,' began Evans.

'It's got to be said,' said Polly Hempseed. 'Personally, unless I can get the reporters to mention me under my real name which, as most of you know, is Conway, I'm in the same boat as Constance. You can't write letters of sob-stuff advice to the lovelorn in a woman's paper and at the same time get yourself tied up in an unsavoury case like this one. I'm with Cassie all the way.'

'Then why don't you marry her?' said Niobe. Everybody looked astounded at the boldness of this uncompromising question.

'*Aren't* you married?' asked Constance.

Latimer Targe tried again.

'With all respect to the chair,' he said, 'I feel I must speak. It is true, Chelion, that poor Miss Minnie did have a claim to this estate and her cousin's money, isn't it?'

I said, 'She had no *legal* claim, Targe.'

'You rat!' said Niobe to Targe. She began to cry.

'You told us you knew, but you didn't tell us how you found out,' said Cassie. (This was all news to me, Dame Beatrice. A nest of vipers was beginning to hatch out.)

'Oh, well, I ferret around, you know,' said Targe, in the

apologetic voice he had used in addressing me. 'I thought Miss Minnie was an interesting old lady and might have something in her past which would make a story if I changed the names of people and places, you know. Miss Kennett *did* say that she thought Miss Minnie must have had a past, and as Miss Kennett was a newspaper woman and reported crime and so forth, I thought perhaps she knew something and that I could track it down. I was rather stuck for material for another book, you see – one is, sometimes – so I poked around and kind of dug up the dirt, you know. Well, that's the way it goes, isn't it?'

'You rat!' said Niobe for the second time. 'Just be quiet! Nobody wants to know.'

CHAPTER 5

The Case for the Police

The meeting broke up in some disorder. Everybody talked at once and Niobe wept. In the end, when he could make himself heard, Evans suggested that we should all hold our horses until we saw how the cat was going to jump and not worry about pigs in pokes until the pigeons headed for home, and with this splendid collection of metaphors he cleared us all out of his sitting-room and settled down, if the sounds were anything to go by, to a first-class row with Constance Kent. At any rate, no more was said about anybody leaving.

The police came again next day, the day of my arrest. They began by taking me through my story, the same story as I have given you, Dame Beatrice, in these pages. If you are going to help me, you had better know the extent of the case against me. I should not have thought it was strong enough to warrant my arrest, but I suppose it must be, as I am now in custody. The police are not anxious to make mistakes.

I think I had better report the interview as I did the previous one; that is, in the form of question and answer, because it is the form the interview took, and a very uncomfortable occasion it was, because I soon perceived that they had only one thought in their heads. They were certain I had killed Miss Minnie and they believed they knew my motive. The means, of course, were obvious. There remained only the question of opportunity, but they had satisfied themselves about that, too.

The main plank in their platform was the fact that Miss Minnie had been a relative of Mrs Dupont-Jacobson. They had been in contact with the lawyers and had found out that Miss Minnie's full name was Minnesota Dupont and that she had been Mrs Dupont-Jacobson's first cousin.

They even admitted that a previous will had named Minnesota Dupont as sole heiress. It turned out, however, that the two women had fallen out when Miss Minnie had joined the Panconscious sect and had promised to leave them her money. Upon this, Mrs Dupont-Jacobson had re-made her will, this time in my favour, so my conversation with the police went as follows:

'Are you sure you knew nothing of Miss Minnie's existence before she came here, sir?'

'I knew nothing of her at all until I returned from Paris. She had then been living in the bungalow here for several months, I believe.'

'Were you surprised when you found out that, apart from a few bequests to charity, you were Mrs Dupont-Jacobson's heir?'

'Naturally I was surprised; overwhelmed, in fact.'

'Did it not occur to you that there might be persons with a better right to the money and the property than yourself?'

'No. Why should it? People have a right to dispose of their own things as they wish.'

'Why did you straightway go to Paris?'

'Why shouldn't I go to Paris?'

'You did not go to escape from claims which were already being made upon you?'

'Certainly not. I went there to get on with a novel I was writing.'

'Yet certain claims had been made. Do not deny this, sir. We have proof.'

'There were a certain number of begging letters. It's like winning the Pools, I suppose. There's always somebody ready to cut himself in for a bit of the stuff.'

'Did one of the letters come from Miss Minnie?'

'Not to my knowledge.'

'How do you mean, sir?'

'When I found I was being pestered, I left instructions that all my correspondence should be examined by Miss Niobe Nutley before it was sent on to Paris. She was to weed out the begging letters and send on only what mattered.'

'Miss Nutley informs us that there was a letter from a Miss Minnesota Dupont among those she sent on to you.'

'If there was, I never got it, but I did change my digs a couple of times in Paris and I don't suppose a concierge at a *pension* would bother about forwarding anything.'

'So you do not deny the possibility that Miss Dupont wrote to you, sir?'

'As a possibility, no, of course I don't. All I can say is that I never received the letter.'

'Did you receive very much correspondence while you were in Paris?'

'Very little; mostly letters from Miss Nutley herself, telling me about the repairs to the house and how the work was progressing.'

'And none of her letters miscarried?'

'Well, she always knew where to find me. I always gave her plenty of notice when I was going to change my address.'

'But in that case, sir, why should Miss Dupont's letter not have reached you? According to what you have just told me, Miss Nutley would have known where to send it. In fact, she would have known what it was, since you had given her instructions to deal with your correspondence and suppress what you refer to as begging letters. Apparently she did not regard Miss Dupont's communication as coming under that heading. Moreover, she asserts that she enclosed it with a letter of her own to explain why she was sending it on.'

'I never received either.'

I may tell you, Dame Beatrice, that at this juncture I asked the Chief Superintendent to send for Niobe, which he was willing to do. I tackled her, but she was absolutely certain that she had sent me Miss Minnie's letter enclosed with one of her own. Pressed by me, she confessed that I had never replied to it, or had ever given any indication that I had received the letter. She then burst into tears and told the police that they must believe me. She repeated this two or three times, which, as you may imagine, did my case no good at all, but Niobe always does overdo things.

Well, they got rid of her with a few soothing words and then turned their attention to me again. A lot of it was a repetition of our earlier interview and referred to keys, window-fastenings and my dips in the sea. They were particularly pressing on the subject of my invasion of Miss Minnie's bungalow, and repeated their question. Why, they asked again, had I taken two men with me and not a woman, if I suspected that Miss Dupont had been taken ill? I repeated my former answer, but they made no secret of the fact that it did not satisfy them.

'You could have taken one of the ladies with you, broken the window and let the lady in at the front door, could you not, sir?'

'I suppose so, if I'd thought of it, but I'm glad I didn't. I wouldn't have wanted a woman to see what was in the bedroom.'

'So you *expected* to find a dead woman!'

'Of course I didn't, but Miss Minnie was elderly, so the thought that she might have died was not so very unlikely.'

This, of course, was all repetition, but I did not change my story. I had no need to, for it was the truth. They tried another tack.

'When you rescued Mrs Dupont-Jacobson from the sea, had you any reason to think that she would reward you?'

'Good Lord, no! Why should she? It was nothing.'

'Your aquatic ability stood her in good stead, sir.'

'Nonsense. There were a dozen fellows, as well as some girls, who could have done what I did. I happened to spot her more quickly, that's all. It wasn't my aquatic ability, as you call it, which mattered much; it was that my job had alerted me to notice swimmers who were in difficulty.'

'When you knew you had inherited this house, sir, what were your ideas concerning it?'

'To sell it. I looked on it as a white elephant.'

'I see. You thought you would realise your assets and live abroad on the proceeds.'

'I had no intention of living abroad permanently.'

'What caused you to visit Miss Dupont's bungalow that morning?'

'What morning?'

'Come, now, sir, don't waste my time.'

'Oh, I see. A parcel had come and the postman had tried several times to deliver it at The Lodge, so, in the end, he brought it to me.'

'And then, sir?'

'I took it across to the bungalow.'

'Immediately?'

'Well, no. I put it down by the hall table and forgot all about it until our cleaner reminded me it was there.'

'So then you took it across, failed to get an answer, returned to get hold of two other gentlemen, Mr Evans and Mr Targe, and broke in. I still don't quite understand why you thought it necessary to break in, sir. Could you not have taken the parcel back to the house and tried again later?'

'Yes, I suppose so, but this wasn't the first time I'd had difficulty in contacting Miss Minnie.'

'Really, sir?'

'Yes. I've remembered what made me so anxious. A few weeks – or it might have been longer than that – yes, I think it was – a registered letter came for her and the postman could get no answer at the Lodge. The thing needed a signature, of course, so he came up to the house and I obliged and promised to see that Miss Minnie got the letter. When I went over there with it – in pouring rain, I might add – I couldn't make anybody hear, so I bunged the envelope through the letter-box and left Miss Minnie to find it.'

'There was no registered envelope among her papers, sir, but that, of course, proves nothing.'

'So when I took the parcel over and couldn't get an answer I began to wonder what was wrong, and that's why I got Evans and Targe to accompany me when I broke in.'

'I see. Now about the anonymous letters. Nobody has shown us any of them.'

'I thought Miss Nutley filed the ones that came for her and me.'

'She claims that she did file them, sir, but that her files had been rifled.'

'Means she was right, then.'

'Right about what, sir?'

'That the ghost scare we had was Miss Minnie snooping around. I told you about that, if you remember. Niobe – Miss Nutley – always thought that it was Miss Minnie.'

'Why did she think so?'

'By that time I think we'd heard that Miss Minnie had been

related to Mrs Dupont-Jacobson and had had – expectations, don't they call them?'

'And was looking for a will of a later date than the one under the terms of which you inherited Weston Pipers, as it is now known, and a very large sum of money?'

'That's what Miss Nutley thought, but, if that's right, the old lady must have been crazy. Actually, I think she was, a bit. They get bees in their bonnets at that age.'

'And water in their lungs, presumably, Mr Piper. I notice that all the main windows of this house face the park and the lake.'

'Yes. It's the best view, so I suppose the architect arranged it that way.'

'So the bungalow, which is on the back lawn, would be unnoticed most of the time.'

'The tradesmen would notice it.'

'And the postman, as you have pointed out. I was thinking of your other tenants.'

'They wouldn't have taken much notice, anyway. As I'm sure I've made clear, Miss Minnie was a recluse. She did not go out, I believe, except for occasional shopping and even for that she refused lifts in people's cars unless Miss Barnes happened to be going her way.'

'So if some ill-disposed person got into the bungalow, overpowered Miss Dupont and dragged her down to the creek and drowned her, especially if this happened at dusk or later, nobody except herself and the murderer need have known anything about it.'

'Except that I should think any old lady so treated would have yelled the place down.'

'Not, perhaps, if she were threatened with a knife or with physical violence, sir.'

'Or if she had a bit of adhesive plaster over her mouth, I suppose,' I said lightly. He gave me the sort of look which I think must be on the face of a cat when finally it pounces upon the mouse it has been playing with. He signalled to his sergeant, who produced a roll of the plaster.

'Strange you should mention it, but we all make mistakes, especially murderers,' he said. But they are wrong, Dame Beatrice. I swear they are wrong. I did not kill Miss Minnie and I have not the slightest idea who did. I can only continue to believe that something in her past life brought about her death and that fate or providence or yourself will take a hand in exonerating me. I never wished her or anybody else any harm. Surely they can't convict me on such evidence as they have? What does it amount to, after all?

I asked them where they had found the plaster, but they said that I knew, as well as they did, where it had been found. I swear that I had no idea there was a roll of the stuff anywhere on the premises, least of all among my own possessions. Can somebody have framed me? It begins to look uncommonly like it. Nest of Vipers! Somebody, joker or not, knew a thing or two when he gave my house that name!

CHAPTER 6

The New Tenant

(1)

'Well, I do not think there is much doubt about who our murderer *could* be,' said Dame Beatrice, 'but proof may be hard to come by and we must not build our case upon theories.'

'It must be one of the people who received the anonymous letters Miss Minnie wrote,' said Laura Gavin, adding an envelope to one of the four neat piles on the breakfast table.

'We have no proof, so far, that Miss Minnie wrote any anonymous letters at all,' Dame Beatrice pointed out.

'But who else would have written them?'

'That remains to be seen, and the letters may have had no importance. The police do not seem to think they had.'

'What shall you do first?'

'I have rented an apartment at Weston Pipers and I shall talk to the people concerned and then look up those previous tenants who have left the house.'

'Do I go with you?'

'Not at the moment. Somebody must remain here to deal with correspondence. I have arranged for George to stay at the bungalow so that I shall not only have my car at my disposal, but a masculine protector if I need one.'

'That will be the day!' said Laura. 'Will George fancy being the tenant of a bungalow which has housed a murdered woman?'

'I have sounded him on the subject and he is eager for the experience.'

'I'd rather him than me.'

'Quite so. I am fortunate in having a factotum who is immune from superstition and who does not believe in ghosts.'

'You'll be careful, won't you?' said Laura rather anxiously.

'As soon as people know that you don't believe this man Piper is guilty, the murderer is going to get a bit restless, don't you think?'

'I shall keep my errand a secret for as long as I can.'

'But you'll have to ask questions and probe into motives and all that.'

'Ah, well, yes, but I shall go as Miss Dorothy L. Sayers's – or, rather, Lord Peter Wimsey's – "lady with a long, woolly jumper on knitting-needles and jingly things round her neck". I shall affect to know nothing of the recent events which have occurred in the house and the bungalow, but merely state that I have answered an advertisement in the local paper. I shall allow it to be understood that I am taking a flat in Weston Pipers as a temporary measure while I am looking for a suitable house of my own in that part of the country.'

'Giving a false name and all that? What fun you are going to have! I'd love to be there and see you in action.'

'That may be sooner than you think, but to begin with I must play a lone hand.'

'Except for George.'

'Except for George. He will take that as his surname. It will be less confusing for both of us if I can continue to refer to him as George, so I have booked him in as William of that ilk, after the famous bookseller.'

'And what shall you call yourself in case I have occasion to write to you or send on any correspondence?'

'You remember my success, perhaps, as Mrs Farintosh at Sir Bohun Chantrey's Sherlock Holmes party some twenty-odd years ago?'

'I hope you don't intend to wear that hideous mixed-tartan rig-out and the elastic-sided boots!'

'That would make me appear eccentric.'

Laura looked at her small, spare, black-eyed, yellow-skinned, beaky-mouthed employer and decided that nature had done all that was necessary to make her look eccentric and that a livelier iris upon the burnished dove would be a redundancy better left unstressed.

'Right. Mrs Farintosh, complete with knitting-needles, it is,' she said, 'and I'll play Sister Ann while you comb through Bluebeard's castle.'

'As a matter of academic interest only, now that you have read Mr Piper's account of the events leading up to his arrest, have you come to any conclusions?' asked Dame Beatrice.

'About the identity of the murderer? Well, the verdict at the inquest was death by drowning, so I agree with you. I don't think Piper is guilty.'

'Interesting. Why do you say that?'

'Because people who have been swimming-bath attendants would never dream of drowning anybody.'

'Surely a sweeping statement?'

'Maybe, but that's my answer and, of course, it stymies me.'

'How so?'

'Because it also lets out the Niobe woman. Apart from this firm belief of mine, I would have picked her as Suspect Number One.'

'Why so?'

'Oh, the old story of the woman scorned, you know. If you look at Piper's evidence objectively, there is nothing to show that this Niobe didn't work the whole thing to bring suspicion on him and land him in the cart as a matter of revenge for his dodging the column and deciding not to marry her.'

'A fascinating theory.'

'But you don't think it's worth the toss of a biscuit.'

'On the contrary, I consider it well-reasoned and most plausible. *Do* people toss biscuits, by the way?'

'To dogs and the birds, perhaps.'

'Rosalind had not one to toss, or, rather, to throw, at a dog. I speak of words, though, not of biscuits. Perhaps she confused the two.'

'And you have not one *or* the other to throw at a bitch. Is that it? For this Niobe, whether she is guilty or not, *is* a bitch. I'm certain of that.'

'Must you malign the poor girl before either of us has so much as met her?'

'If she isn't a bitch, why hasn't this Piper married her? He seems, by his own account, to have intended marriage when he could afford it. Why would he have ducked out as soon as fortune favoured him?'

'He explains that, I think. While he was a poor man he was

safe from the toils. As soon as he became wealthy his bulwark was gone.'

'So we write him off for a heel and join in Niobe's tears, do we?'

'I have better use for my eyes than to redden them in a lost cause.'

'But you don't think Piper's is a lost cause?'

'If I did, I should not be undertaking this enquiry. I propose to begin by supposing that Piper has told the truth and nothing but the truth.'

'But not necessarily the whole truth. Is that the size of it?'

'Nobody would dare to tell the *whole* truth about *anything*, even if he knew it,' said Dame Beatrice.

(2)

Weston Pipers, Dame Beatrice thought, when, having stepped out of the car, she surveyed it before ringing the bell, was a gracious, benign old house. It was made of rose-coloured brick with facings of grey stone, long windows and a porch which was pillared, recently repaired and unlikely to have been a feature of the original building. Yet it was not entirely out of place since it was well-proportioned and its grey colouring matched the facings of the house.

The doorbell was answered by a young woman whom Dame Beatrice rightly took to be the Niobe of Piper's narrative. She was tall, well-built with a fully-matured figure and, as her half-sleeved dress displayed, remarkably powerful forearms.

'You will be Mrs Farintosh. Do come in,' she said. 'I'll show you straight up to your flat and then I'll let your man into the bungalow. Not too many stairs for you, I hope? The first-floor flats are occupied, so I've had to put you on the second floor, but the rooms are quite large and if you're nervous about fire – some people are – you will find that an iron fire-escape staircase is just to the right of your door.'

Dame Beatrice followed her up a broad, beautiful oak staircase and then up a second one which was narrower and less expensively carpeted. The young woman produced two keys. One she handed to Dame Beatrice; the other – a master-

key Dame Beatrice supposed – she applied to the door in front
of her at the top of the stairs.

'The doors are self-locking, I suppose,' said Dame Beatrice.

'Oh, yes, but if you lock yourself out by accident and have
left your key inside, I can always let you in.'

'I hope there are inside bolts on the doors. Twice in my own
home I have been troubled with intruders.'

'Oh, dear! Burglars, do you mean?'

'Luckily they did not get away with whatever it was they
had come for.' (Dame Beatrice did not add that on both
occasions it had been her life, not her goods, which the
intruders had sought to take away.)

'It must have made you very nervous.'

'Well, a little cautious, perhaps.' She looked at the inside of
the opened door. 'Oh, no bolts, I see.'

'I'm afraid not. We have had people here living on their
own, so, in case of emergency – illness, you know – it would be
necessary to break the door down to reach them and help
them if inside bolts were used. But this house is amply secure.
There are bolts inside the back and front doors and patent
fastenings on all the downstair windows. We are quite
impregnable, I assure you.'

The flat consisted of a sitting-room, bedroom, small kitchen
and even smaller bathroom, but the windows overlooked the
park and gardens and the bathroom window, when its frosted
casement was opened, gave a view of the front lawn, the
bungalow and the tiny inlet.

'Splendid,' said Dame Beatrice.

'I thought you would like it. It is not completely furnished
because our long-stay tenants like to bring their own bits and
pieces with them, but I think you will be able to manage with
what there is, as you will only be here for a week or two.'

'Oh, I am sure I can manage. It all looks very pleasant and
comfortable.'

'The last tenants were two girls, so they took quite good care
of the furniture except that, as they were both heavy smokers, I
had to have all the curtains cleaned when they went, and new
chair-covers made to hide the cigarette-burns. I don't know
why women smokers are so abominably careless. I would have
seen to it that they paid for the curtains and the damage, but

they went off at such short notice, leaving no forwarding address, that the house had to bear the expense.'

'Which meant you yourself, I suppose,' said Dame Beatrice. Niobe did not answer except with a laugh and a shrug of her powerful shoulders. ('She certainly is not going to explain that the owner of the house is in prison and awaiting trial for murder,' thought Dame Beatrice, 'and small blame to her!')

George, waiting at the front door, insisted upon relieving Niobe of Dame Beatrice's suitcases, and then put the car away before being shown his own quarters. Dame Beatrice joined him and Niobe at the front door of the bungalow, where Niobe was vainly attempting to turn the key in the lock. George tried in his turn, but in vain.

'How strange!' said Niobe. 'I had better go back to the house for the key which the police took from the body.'

When she had returned and let them in:

'Will you be comfortable here, George?' asked Dame Beatrice, as soon as Niobe had gone.

'Oh, yes, madam, very comfortable. I have had lessons from Henri, madam, and am in a position to cook for you if you will allow me into your apartment for the purpose.'

'I have a better idea, George. I will come over here for my meals and you shall cook for both of us. Your kitchen is larger than mine and has an electric cooker which, if you have been Henri's pupil, you will know how to handle. It will mean that we can compare notes without appearing to conspire together.'

'Very good, madam. At what time do you choose to dine this evening? I have all the provisions in the boot of the car.'

'At about eight, do you think? Breakfast I will manage for myself, as I require nothing but toast and coffee. Lunch we will take most days at a hotel in the town. I have to keep up a pretence of house hunting.'

'Very good, madam.' He accompanied her to the front door. She inspected it.

'No bolts, George, I see.'

'No, the place is hardly burglar-proof, madam.'

('Nor murderer-proof,' thought Dame Beatrice.) 'If you were moved to drown somebody at the bottom of the lawn, George,' she said to him, 'would you take the trouble to carry

the body back to this bungalow and then indulge in the
pleasure of smashing it over the head?'

'That, in any case, seems unnecessary, madam, if the body
was already a dead one. Possibly the murderer would not have
been certain that life was already extinct, though.'

'I have an idea that this particular murderer knew all the
tests to make sure of that, George.'

'Then the assault on the head seems to have been super-
fluous, madam.'

'Or merely an act of sheer spitefulness, but, in that case, I
wonder why? But it is the risk the murderer took in bringing
the body back from the water which has worried me from the
beginning.'

'Is it certain that the victim was drowned in the sea,
madam? This bungalow has a bathroom with a full-sized bath
in it.'

'The body had drowned in sea water. There was sea water
(tested) in the lungs and a small piece of seaweed was found on
the body. All the same, I am sure you are right. She was not
drowned in the sea. Now that I have seen this place I am
convinced of that.'

(3)

The invitation to take mid-morning coffee with Constance
Kent came as a surprise until Dame Beatrice realised that she
was to be the recipient of confidences of a kind which could
not be disclosed in front of Evesham Evans, Constance's
husband. His temporary absence – he had gone to the bank to
draw out some money, his wife explained – gave Constance a
chance to unburden herself and she took full advantage of it.
The fact of police surveillance, dwelt on with bitter indigna-
tion by the torrid novelist, suggested to Dame Beatrice that the
case of the police against Chelion Piper was not as strong as
they would have liked it to be and that they were half-
expecting a Micawber-like something to turn up, a something
which might well cause them to revise their first opinion that
Chelion was a murderer.

Having expressed herself forcibly on the subject of police inter-
ference with the rights of British citizens, Constance went on:

'Of course, nobody believes that Chelion murdered that wretched woman.' At Dame Beatrice's well-simulated look of surprise, she gave an account of the circumstances which had overtaken Weston Pipers.

'Then why is he under arrest?' asked Dame Beatrice innocently.

'Well, Evesham thinks it's just a ruse, you know.'

'A ruse?'

'Oh, my dear Mrs Farintosh, the police are up to all kinds of tricks these days. Evesham says that the real murderer thinks he is perfectly safe and so he'll do some stupid thing or other and give the game away. Poor Chelion – such a nice, modest, unassuming fellow and so much liked by everybody – is just a stool-pigeon, Evesham says.'

'Your husband appears to have given a great deal of thought to the matter.'

'Well, of course, he was there with Chelion and that sinister man Latimer Targe when they found her body, you know. Targe made off at once on the excuse of telephoning the doctor and the police, but *I* always think there is something very underhand and unpleasant about a man who earns his living by *wallowing in crime*.'

'Oh? How does Mr Targe do that?'

'He looks up and writes up real-life murder cases, but, of course, a person of *your* education and breeding – it's easy to tell the *real sort* when you meet them, isn't it? – would never dream of touching his books.'

'*Risqué?*' asked Dame Beatrice in a low and horrified tone.

'Worse, my dear. After all, sex is a perfectly natural thing, whatever strange antics it may get up to, as I try to explain in my novels. Not that I could ever approve or countenance the path pursued by those two young women who left us just about the time of Miss Minnie's death.'

'Oh, dear me! You found their conduct shocking?'

'Yes, indeed. Such strange goings-on! I believe the Greeks had a word for it, but *I* simply call it unhealthy. And the names they choose to be known by! Billie, for instance. Why could she not write under the name of Wilhelmina, which must have been how she was christened, if indeed she was christened at all. And the other one, Elysée, when of course her real name is simple, undistinguished Elsie! I wonder she did not call herself Désirée and have done with it.'

'So you got rid of them?'

'My dear, I had to insist that Miss Nutley did. They were a *most* undesirable pair. Besides, Evesham had begun making what used to be called sheep's eyes at Elysée. Never, Mrs Farintosh, be persuaded to marry a man younger than yourself.'

'I was not so persuaded and the chance is unlikely to be presented to me now.'

'Ah, well, I spoke rhetorically. I made that mistake and have regretted it for years. My marriage, Mrs Farintosh, has not been a happy or an easy one.'

Dame Beatrice said she was sorry to hear it, but she supposed that nobody's life was a bed of roses.

'You may wonder,' Constance went on, rightly ignoring this deplorable cliché, 'why I write the kind of novels I do. With my undoubted talents I could have done anything, simply anything I chose, Mrs Farintosh.'

Dame Beatrice said that Thomas Gray had been so right, so very right.

'Thomas Gray? You mean Gray of *Gray's Elegy*?'

Yes, Dame Beatrice had meant Gray of *Gray's Elegy*. (It sounded like some owner of a stately home open to the public at fifty pence a time, she thought.) She quoted:

'Full many a flower is born to blush unseen,
And waste its sweetness on the desert air.'

Constance Kent did not appear to be flattered.

'That is hardly *me*,' she said. 'I certainly was not "born to blush unseen".'

'Ah,' said Dame Beatrice, 'perhaps, then, you see yourself as:

Some village Whitehouse who, with dauntless breast,
The pornographic tyranny withstood;
Some mute inglorious Joan of Arc may rest,
Some Corday guiltless of foul Marat's blood.'

'I don't recollect that Gray wrote those words,' said Constance, looking puzzled.

Dame Beatrice waved a yellow claw. 'I was attempting to

rescue the poet from the charge of being a male chauvinist pig,' she said.

'Oh, dear! I am not a Women's Libber, Mrs Farintosh, and *that*,' said Constance, looking happier, 'brings me back to Kennett and Barnes.'

'You said you got rid of them.'

'I got the idea from a letter which was actually sent to me myself – anonymously, of course. Well, you know, all is grist which comes to a novelist's mill, so although the letter was very unpleasant both in content and in the unpleasant words it used, I thought *Why Not?*'

'Why not what?'

'Write one myself, of course. I was stuck in the fourth chapter of my *Split Summer* – Split being that place on the Dalmatian coast, so it was rather a clever title, I thought – but somehow I had come to a full stop. Then came this letter. It horrified me at first, but then I suddenly saw how to open up my book. I am, of course, a purist where my work is concerned, so I wanted to find out for myself what effect an anonymous letter was likely to have on the recipient.'

'But I thought you knew the effect such a letter had on the recipient. You say you yourself had received one.'

'I am hardly a typical case. I knew that the statements and accusations contained in my letter were lies. The letter I wrote to these two misguided girls was the truth.'

'May I ask—?'

'What was in the letter I myself received? Certainly. I have nothing to hide. The letter accused me of having trapped Evesham into marrying me and it enquired, in a most disagreeable way, how I had managed it. My reply, I should explain, was only tit for tat. I knew where my letter came from. Kennett and Barnes wrote it.'

'What made you decide that it came from those two girls?'

'Oh, my dear! They were quite, *quite* abnormal.'

'You destroyed the letter, I suppose.'

'You may be sure I did! Even if I had not, I would not dream of showing it to you. However, I retaliated in kind and – talk about killing two birds with one stone! – my novel suddenly took fire again and those two embarrassing and *dangerous* young women lost their nerve and spent no time at all in packing their bags and leaving. I told Miss Nutley what I had done and she undertook to see that they got the anonymous letter.'

'You were going to tell me what makes you write your novels.'

'Oh, that, yes. Well, for one thing, I want to leave the world a better place than it was when I entered it. I am a moral reformer, Mrs Farintosh.'

'A moral reformer?'

'My dearest wish is to do good.'

'Robert Louis Stevenson thought it was more necessary to *be* good.'

'Oh, well, I suppose one takes "being good" for granted. I am sure *I* have nothing with which to reproach myself.'

'Stevenson went further. Not only did he think he had to be good; he thought he had no duty to make his neighbour good, but to make him happy, if that were possible.'

'I have made thousands happy in my time,' said Constance complacently. 'It is my aim to brighten the drab lives of other women. Deprived of happiness myself, I also write by way of compensation, I suppose, for my unfulfilled, unsatisfactory married life.' The story of Constance Kent's unhappy, unsatisfactory married life lasted for the ensuing hour, but Dame Beatrice, listening patiently to the garbled and, she was sure, highly-exaggerated history of Constance Kent's wrongs, felt that the time had not been wasted. At least the author of one of the anonymous letters was now known, and the letter itself reason enough to explain, perhaps, the abrupt departure of Billie and Elysée. Later on, she decided, she would ask Constance Kent to reproduce the document.

(4)

As though Constance Kent had set a fashion, two more invitations had been pushed under Dame Beatrice's sitting-room door while she was at lunch. One was from Mandrake Shard suggesting tea for two at a little place he knew not far from Weston Pipers. As the other invitation was for cocktails with Polly Hempseed and Cassie McHaig at six in the evening, she was able to accept both.

She had expected, from Piper's written description, that Mandrake Shard would be a small man, but, even so, she was slightly taken aback when he knocked gently on her door at half-past three that afternoon. She was accustomed to be dwarfed by Laura and by Laura's husband and tall son, and by her own son, Sir Ferdinand Lestrange. She found it almost a unique experience to find herself playing giantess to a man whose height she estimated at well under five feet.

Mandrake Shard was not mis-shapen. Except that his head was rather too large for his body, he was quite well-proportioned.

'I often walk to this farm place for my tea,' he explained, 'but you won't want to do that in this wintry weather. I've brought my car round. I had to have a few adjustments made to accommodate my height, you know' – he spoke as though he were nine feet tall instead of about half that – 'but I'm a very good driver, I assure you – careful, you know, and courteous to other drivers and, of course, I do understand my car. We go everywhere together.' He gave a falsetto little giggle. 'Her name is Portia, because she's got gaskets. Do you see the joke? Portia of Belmont, Italy, had caskets. Portia of Weston Pipers, England, has gaskets. Clever, don't you think?'

Dame Beatrice, seating herself beside him in the front of the car, agreed that it was very clever. She added that it was also most amusing.

'Ah, now, talking about amusing,' said Shard, steering the car through the gateway and turning left on to a narrow road, 'I really must tell you of a *most* amusing thing I did – really one of my very best efforts. I get hold of a good deal of information by listening at doors, you know. I write rather good spy stories, as perhaps you know, so listening at doors and looking through keyholes is part of my stock-in-trade. Helps me to get the right atmosphere into my books, so I don't look upon it as common or garden snooping—'

'Although others might think there was a resemblance,' Dame Beatrice pointed out, as he seemed to expect some comment at this stage of his narrative.

'Oh, I've been assaulted, you know, punched and kicked. Once I was kicked from top to bottom of a long, steep staircase. But the way I look at it is that it's all in a secret service agent's life-cycle and it helps me to get the feel of things.' He gave his high-pitched little giggle again. 'Did you notice I said "feel"? I was black and blue for a week!'

'You appear to make real sacrifices to your art,' said Dame Beatrice.

'That's what art is for – to have sacrifices made to it. Art is a god, you know, and a god demands sacrifices, oh, dear me, yes.'

'You were going to tell me about one of your best jokes,' Dame Beatrice reminded him, certain that she was going to be told the origin of Nest of Vipers. So it proved. He had overheard a conversation between Piper and Niobe and had managed to exchange their order to the printer for one of his own.

'It was a perfectly simple matter,' he went on, with another falsetto giggle. 'Outgoing letters are placed on the hall table just as is the incoming mail, so all I had to do was to abstract the envelope addressed to the printers, substitute my own missive for Piper's order for the new stationery, and off the letters went as usual. Our excellent charwoman picks them up, you know, and posts them on her way home.'

'A simple matter indeed,' Dame Beatrice agreed, 'and the result, I suppose, amused everybody.'

'Well, I am not sure about Chelion and Niobe. Everybody else thought it a good joke.'

'Chelion?'

'Chelion Piper.'

'He had to pay for your joke, I suppose.'

'Well, I could hardly own up to it, could I? – especially now I know what he's capable of doing if anybody angers him.'

'Oh? Of what is he capable?'

'Murder, no less. I was there when Targe came into the house to telephone the police. I saw him come tearing across from the bungalow and I'd seen Piper and Evans go across there with him, so, of course, I listened outside the office door and heard him ask for a doctor and then he phoned for the police.'

'I have heard something of this from Mrs Constance Kent.'

'You should say *Miss* Constance Kent. Professional women who use a pseudonym are always deemed to be unmarried.'

'I am obliged to you for the information. What makes you think that Mr Piper committed murder?'

'Oh, Miss Minnie wrote anonymous letters, you know. Such a wicked and dangerous thing to do.'

'How do you know she wrote them?'

'Well, the letters came and she was murdered. One only has to put two and two together.'

'But can you be sure that Mr Piper received an anonymous letter?'

'Oh, yes, he had at least one such missive, I think. If he hadn't, he wouldn't have murdered her, would he? I'll tell you something else, too. I know Minnie sometimes had a man in that bungalow at night.'

'Oh, really, who was that?'

'I don't know. I am not tall enough to look in at the windows. I'd heard the voice before, but I couldn't place it.'

'So it wasn't Mr Piper's voice?'

'Doesn't prove he isn't a murderer.'

'Did *you* receive a letter?' asked Dame Beatrice, abandoning the game of going round in circles. Shard did not answer until he had parked his car and they were seated at the tea table in a cottage where the owner's wife (he informed Dame Beatrice proudly) did all her own baking.

'Yes,' he said, 'I got one of the letters. I can't show it you because I destroyed it. It was unkind, but not scurrilous. It called me Jack the Giant-killer and asked what I had done with my beanstalk.'

'That does not sound very unkind.'

'I don't know how Miss Minnie knew,' said Shard, 'but I was once engaged to a girl a good deal taller than myself. I broke the engagement because my friends, so-called, were so – well, they thought it a subject for coarse humour.'

'People are very insensitive.'

'Insensitive? Yes, one could say that, I suppose. Are you a Sensitive, Mrs Farintosh?'

'I thought it was an adjective, not a noun. What is a Sensitive?'

'I see you do not understand me. I had an idea that you were One of Us.'

'You still appear to use capital letters. One of whom?'

'Ah, well, obviously you do not understand. You don't belong to the Panconscious People, do you?' A waitress came up to the small table and, after consultation with his guest, Shard ordered and said nothing more until the tea arrived. Dame Beatrice took advantage of his silence (which was not absolute, for he was humming very softly, regardless of the indignant glare of a woman who was seated at the next table) to work out the meaning of his last question. He returned to it as soon as the tea was poured, but by that time she was ready for him.

'The Panconscious People,' she said, 'sound both strange and sinister. Pan is a terrifying and unpredictable god. One remembers a story by E.M. Forster.'

'Oh, I'm sure these people are sinister. I went, you know, but it alarmed me very much. Our own practices are pure and are for the benefit of mankind. Theirs are evil. Exciting, intoxicating, but - oh, yes. evil. So you are not a witch?'

'I am a psychiatrist.'

'Ah, then, to that extent, you are a Believer.'

'In what?'

'In the Power.'

'Of witchcraft?'

'In the power of the occult. In the power of some minds over others. In the power of the Old Gods.'

'With reservations, yes, I ascribe power to all those things, but whether one should meddle with them is another matter entirely. Aspirations, ideals and forms of worship may be excellent in themselves, but my work has led me to the conclusion that there can be a very narrow line between some forms of worship and some forms of mental instability - to put it as mildly as possible.'

'Yes, I know what you mean. I think some of the others have crossed that narrow line. I would not have thought Piper was one of them, though. It just shows how difficult it is to know what people really are like. Will you take more tea?'

'Thank you. By the way, I am invited to cocktails this evening.'

'Polly Hempseed and Cassie McHaig, yes. I shall be there. but I don't drink. Still, I shall go.'

(5)

It turned out that all the tenants of Weston Pipers had been invited. They included the newly-returned Irelath Moore and his charming little companion, Sumatra. Mandrake Shard was present, as he had said he would be, and his tiny frame was installed at a table in a corner of the room well away from the cocktail bar which occupied the whole of one long wall. A coffee-pot and a plate of sweet biscuits were on a smaller table beside Shard and he appeared to be enjoying himself, for he waved a biscuit cheerily at Dame Beatrice as she entered, and called out, 'Meet the gang!'

Polly Hempseed proved to be a charming and courteous host, Cassie McHaig an assiduous and capable hostess and the party went well. Except that it gave her an opportunity of seeing all the tenants together, however, the evening was wasted from Dame Beatrice's point of view, since what she had hoped for was to have a word in private with Hempseed and Cassie.

As, on this occasion, there was no opportunity for so doing, she amused herself by studying the company, chatting with this one and that and noting the by-plays and inter-relationships which, under the influence of the blushful Hippocrene, gradually began to manifest themselves. Particularly she became aware that her hostess was keeping not only a watchful eye but also an alert and suspicious ear (difficult though it must have been to do so amid the clack of almost a dozen shrill or booming literary voices, each aggressively eager to assert itself against all comers) upon her husband (or whatever he might be). The tall, handsome, debonair Polly Hempseed seemed to combine the attitudes and easy self-assurance of a man of the world with the equally easy charm and unsophisticated attractiveness of a well-mannered under-graduate, and it was not at all difficult to see why the homely, downright, superficially unglamorous Cassie had not only chosen him for a life-partner, but was accustomed to keep eye and ear on him.

It was almost impossible to conjecture why *he* had selected *her* to live with, thought Dame Beatrice.

'She's up to his weight,' said Latimer Targe, as though he had read her thoughts. 'You're wondering about our host and hostess, aren't you? So did I when I first met them. It's the old story of the immovable whatever it is and the irresistible something else. They are for ever locked in a useless and exhausting struggle for supremacy. They can't overcome one another and that means they can't get away from one another. We see a lot of it in our business, you know.'

'In *your* business?'

'The literary battle ground. Passionate friends who'd give anything for a chance to part but are held together as a magnet holds a collection of iron filings; deadly enemies whose *raison d'être* would dissolve like the dew on the grass if they ceased to have one another to contend with. The whole world of art and letters is a seething cauldron, Mrs Farintosh. You may well regret having entered it.'

'I wonder whether Miss Minnie regretted having entered it?' said Dame Beatrice.

'I believe she was already in it. She edited some esoteric journal for some off-beat religious community, you know. It wouldn't surprise me in the least if one of the congregation did her in for expressing subversive views in her editorials. These off-beat sects are a pretty weird lot, in my opinion.'

'You have attended the meetings of Miss Minnie's particular group, perhaps?'

'Once and once only. Shard took me. He said (having a bee in his bonnet, poor little runt) that they were a ring of spies. *My* impression was that they *could* be a gang of crooks and that Minnie was their stool-pigeon and had been sent here to case the joint and see who was worth robbing.'

'Dear me! What bizarre ideas appear to be current in the literary world!'

'Oh, we're all mad nor' nor' west, I expect,' said Latimer, 'and, of course, the Pans may not be criminals at all; just a collection of dim-witted freaks with a proselytising mission and no sense of humour.'

'Oh, they make converts, do they?'

'Not so's you notice. At any rate they didn't make a convert of *me*. I don't know whether Shard ever went again, but I don't suppose he did.'

Another lynx-eyed member of the assemblage (not surprisingly in view of her disclosures) was Constance Kent, for although Elysée Barnes was not at the party, the lovely, doll-like, brilliant, tiny Sumatra was. Sumatra was like a butterfly, Dame Beatrice thought. She was flitting from one person or group to another, smiling, bowing, chattering.

When he could manage it, the taciturn, scowling, black-a-vised, jealous Irelath, who had been watching her every movement, gathered her up at last and planted her on his knee where, without any self-consciousness, as contented as a child who knows she is loved, she snuggled up against him and only raised her head from his shoulder to be given sips out of his glass.

'*That* relationship is at least *normal*,' said Constance Kent.

At seven-fifteen, as the party showed no sign whatever of breaking up and Cassie brought in more refreshments and Polly poured out more drinks, Dame Beatrice said goodnight and went to her room to change for dinner. There had been one slightly disconcerting moment at the party. Introduced to her at its beginning, Irelath Moore had stared, scowled, stared harder, smiled with infinite charm and then said:

'Mrs Farintosh? Married again, have you?'

CHAPTER 7

Personal Questions

(1)

'It may turn out to be rather a nuisance, George, if Mr Moore has recognised me,' she said, as George waited on her at table that same evening. 'I may have to take him into my confidence, and that is the last thing I want to do with anybody in that house, with the exception, I think, of Mr Evesham Evans.'

'Would a face of brass and a policy of stout denial meet the case of Mr Moore, madam?'

'I doubt it. He may be a poet in his own right, but he is also the son of a business man who went to Canada with almost nothing and now is a cattle baron. I do not think it would be easy to hoodwink him, and it might lead to unnecessary complications if I did.'

As it chanced, she had no need to contact Irelath, for he tapped at her door on the following morning and said:

'Excuse the early call, but I knew you were up. I saw you go down to the hall for your letters. You wouldn't care to put me wise, would you?'

'I think you had better come in, Mr Moore,' said Dame Beatrice. When she had admitted him, she added, 'As you appear to surmise, there are reasons why we should not converse upon landings. There is also a good reason for keeping our voices low and for our seating ourselves as far as possible from the door.'

'I get you,' said Irelath, relaxing his long frame in the arm-chair which she indicated and his habitual expression to a grin of tolerant understanding. 'The eyes and ears of this place are four feet six in height and have a complex about spies. Right?'

'Right. Well, now, ask your question. It was good of you not to elaborate upon it last night.'

'Oh, it is nothing to do with me if you change your name. Most of the folk here have changed theirs and, like you, I am sure, for the best of reasons.'

'I am Mrs Farintosh only while I live here. Does that convey anything to you?'

'Well, at a guess, I'd say you were here to look into the matter of the old lady's death. That means you're not sure Chelion Piper did for her.'

'I keep an open mind. What is your own opinion?'

'The one I gave the police when they came rooting around and questioned us. That bloke didn't hold any old lady under water and drown her. Still less did he bash her over the head afterwards.'

'She is said to have written some anonymous letters. Such letters can be hurtful and even dangerous.'

'Sure. I got one myself. One was sent to my baby, too, but as in the ordinary way she never gets any letters—'

'Not even from her editor?'

'Bless you, she hasn't got an editor. *I'm* Sumatra, except for the photograph at the top of the page. Su can't write a word of English. She just gives me the low-down and I write it up. Simple as that.'

'So when this anonymous letter came?'

'I opened it as usual and found out it was some more of this pernicious muck about our not being married. Well, we *are* married, to all intents and purposes. What do a few formal words said in front of witnesses and the scribble on a dirty little piece of paper matter? I shall always stick to Su and she will always stick to me. I don't keep an eye on *her*, you know, only on the fellows who'd like to muscle in on my patch. I'll kill if I have to. Simple as that.'

'Simplicity appears to be your strong suit, Mr Moore.'

'Sure. With Su and me it's like the old song says: *I know where I'm going, and I know who's going with me.*'

'It goes on: *I know whom I love, but the Dear knows whom I'll marry.*'

'I shall never marry except in one eventuality, so let the Dear look after his own.'

'His own, perhaps – or one of them – being Miss Minnie's murderer?'

'You said it. Simple as that. You know, Dame – OK Mrs Farintosh – I don't understand about that old lady's death. She was a bit off-beat, maybe even a little loose from the neck up, but I'll swear she was harmless.'

'The anonymous letters?'

'Phooee! I don't believe she wrote nary a one of 'em.'

'Have you any grounds for that belief?'

Irelath grinned.

'I haven't the sort of proof a policeman would accept, but you might be willing to consider it. I guess that poor little runt Shard wrote them.'

'There appears to be one, at least, which he did not write.'

'Oh? Which would that be?'

'The letter or, as I think, letters, which got Miss Kennett and Miss Barnes out of the house.'

'Oh, you know about them, do you? That damned woman Constance Kent, I suppose, going all orthodox and righteous. Well, her heaven-made marriage doesn't seem to go so very well. I suppose she couldn't stand the sight of two people who could get on together. I suspect her of having had a go at Sumatra and me, but, although I tackled her, she denied it, and I could have been wrong.'

'So what makes you think of Mr Shard?'

'He's a devious, listening-at-keyholes little bit of nonsense, and he's got a permanent chip on his shoulder because of his lack of inches. But about poor old Minnie. Why should anybody kill her?'

'The answer to that lies in what has been called "the psychology of the individual".'

'Well, that's up your street rather than mine. Too bad, though, that Piper has to take the rap. Are you going to winkle him out of it?'

'Your metaphors are deplorably mixed.'

'It's the Irish in me. Say, when you're free, will you come to lunch with Su and me? She dishes up something pretty special in the way of a curry.'

(2)

'To sum up' (wrote Dame Beatrice to Laura) 'the consensus of opinion here is that Chelion Piper is innocent. So far, I have come upon no evidence to show that this majority verdict is either right or wrong, I went to lunch yesterday with Irelath and Sumatra, ate a fearful and wonderful meal prepared and cooked by the latter and had further speech with Irelath while she was doing the washing-up. It was he who gave me the general opinion, but, of course, he may be mistaken.

'This morning I issued my own invitation to Cassie McHaig and Mr Hempseed for cocktails in the bungalow. George will act as barman. My invitation has been accepted, so I will let you know later if any developments ensue. I have yet to talk to these two privately and also I want to see Mr Evans when his wife is not present.

'After that, it will be necessary to trace Miss Kennett and Miss Barnes. I have been given (by Irelath Moore) the name of the newspaper for which Miss Kennett works, so it should not be a difficult matter to find out her new address. Irelath recognised me, but has remained most discreet about my identity. It seems that he was among my audience at a lecture somewhere or other. He further informs me that if Sumatra becomes pregnant he will marry her at once in case his "old man cuts up rough and acts sticky" about his inheritance. This statement was followed by what appears to be his verbal signature (if there can be such a thing; you may prefer to call it his signature tune). This consists of the words: "It's as simple as that." He added that if I recollected our previous conversation he would like to add that any stick will do if one intends to beat a dog. So far, I am of his opinion that Chelion Piper has been what the criminal classes call "framed".

'Opinions about Miss Minnie, incidentally, vary, but that is to be expected. After I have talked with the inhabitants past and present of Weston Pipers I must find out more about her from those who were part of her life before she took up residence in the bungalow. When I have seen the rest of the tenants, and before I interview these "outsiders", I shall talk with Miss Niobe Nutley. She strikes me as a formidable young woman who will want to know (in your own phrase) what the hell I am up to, as, of course, these probings of mine must reach a point where they will be regarded as something more significant than the idle curiosity of a nose-poking old woman.'

(3)

Apart from the satisfaction which comes from returning hospitality, Dame Beatrice gained little from entertaining Cassie McHaig and Polly Hempseed. For one thing, they had quarrelled and at first found it difficult to be even civil to one another. Apart from that, it soon became clear that neither believed Chelion Piper to be guilty and both thought Miss Minnie to have written the anonymous letters. These, both were convinced, were what had led to her death, although neither was prepared to name her murderer.

'Stands to reason,' said Hempseed, swallowing his drink and reaching out for another, 'that the police have fixed on Piper. After all, we know nothing of his life before he took over Nest of Vipers – yes, it *is* still funny and I shall call it that, Cassie, if I choose – except that he had lived for a year in Paris. In *Paris!* Well, I ask you! I bet he collected enough of a past there to last him a lifetime and somehow or other the police guess that Minnie got to know about it. Suppose he wronged her daughter—'

'Oh, keep your sob-stuff for your Answers to Correspondents!' said Cassie.

'Stranger things have happened than people wronging other people's daughters. You should see some of the letters I get. Heartrending!' said Hempseed, pulling a face at her.

'Nonsense! Just like to see themselves in print, that's all. I've no patience with people who make a parade of their troubles.'

'Not a parade of their troubles. A safety-valve for their emotions, if you like.'

'All right, so long as you think so,' said Cassie. 'I'll tell you who *could* do with a safety-valve for her emotions and that's Niobe. She frets for Chelion. She may look like a taller edition of Lola Sapola, but she's a pushover where Chelion is concerned. *That's* a sob-story if you like.'

'If you ask *me*, it's not Niobe's *emotions* that need an outlet. *I* think she's gone off her rocker,' said Hempseed.

'Oh, rubbish! She's as sane as you are,' snapped Cassie.

'Then why has she taken to walking about at night disturbing and frightening people? She's got this master-key, which means she can get in anywhere. I don't like it.'

'I wonder you don't have bolts put on your doors,' said Dame Beatrice. 'That, surely, would be the answer if you don't want nocturnal visitors.'

'It would if she would allow it, but she won't,' said Hempseed. 'Says it would spoil the beautiful woodwork.'

'Perhaps she should be confronted with a *fait accompli*.'

'Put bolts on the doors without asking permission?' said Cassie. 'The next thing would be our notice to quit.'

'I wanted to put a chair against the door at night,' said Hempseed, 'but madam here said that at least Niobe moved around quietly, whereas the chair would make a row if she shoved against it trying to get in. But then Niobe's walkabouts at night don't wake madam up. It's only poor old light-sleeper me who gets disturbed.'

'How often does she pay these visits?' asked Dame Beatrice.

'I don't know about other people, but she has opened our door twice in the past ten days.'

'What can be her object, I wonder?'

'Just restlessness, I guess,' said Cassie, 'and perhaps nosiness about people sleeping together. I would say she has a fairly nasty mind, but I'm very sorry for her.'

'We share a bed,' said Hempseed, 'being married and all that. I know it's old-fashioned nowadays, but we tied ourselves up without thinking.'

'*I* thought,' said Cassie. 'I come of Presbyterian stock and have my prejudices. Of course nobody *here* knows that we're married, so we'd be glad if you kept it dark. Evesham and Constance don't mind being known as a married couple, but we think in the modern way.'

'Did you receive any of the anonymous letters which appear to have been distributed to some of the residents?'

'Yes, we had a couple – one each. Why?'

'You have not kept them, of course?'

'We did at first,' said Cassie, 'because we thought of going to the police, but when old Minnie was killed we knew that it would be unnecessary, so then we destroyed them.'

'Were you so sure that Miss Minnie wrote them?'

'Well, nobody has had one since she went. We always thought she wrote them, but when no more came it seemed like proof.'

'When Miss Nutley entered your bedroom, what did she do?'

'Nothing,' replied Hempseed. 'When I sat up and switched on the light she murmured that she was sorry she'd mistaken the room. Very funny that she mistook it twice!'

'You never wondered whether she and not Miss Minnie wrote the letters?'

'We might have done,' said Cassie, 'but when she had one herself she asked every one of us except Latimer Targe, who doesn't own a typewriter, to turn out a half-page of typing for us all to compare with the typing on her letter and on any which we had received.'

'People made no secret of the fact that they had received these communications, then?'

'Oh, no. Nobody here is particularly reticent about private matters except the two girls who have left. I believe everybody had at least one letter, except Evesham and Constance,' said Hempseed.

'And if we'd let it be known that we were married, instead of letting people think we are just living together, I don't believe *we* would have had one,' said Cassie. 'That's what *I* think. Minnie was just the kind of old party who would think cohabitation outside marriage was the blackest of sins. She worked for some peculiar religious group, you know.'

'And did people co-operate by producing their specimens of typing?' asked Dame Beatrice.

'Everybody except Miss Minnie. There, according to Niobe, she met with a point-blank refusal. Latimer Targe even produced a page which his typist had done for him. Niobe had talked about bringing the police in, you see, so we all thought the sensible thing was to put ourselves in the clear.'

'And the typings did not match with the typing of the anonymous letters?'

'We even used a magnifying glass and they didn't. Mind you, Chelion bought Niobe a new typewriter just about that time.'

'But you assumed that Miss Minnie wrote the letters?'

'She was the kind of queer old party who would,' said Hempseed.

'No mention was made at the inquest about a typewriter being found in the bungalow after Miss Minnie's death,' said Cassie, 'but that proves nothing. She would have got rid of it as soon as there was talk about sending for the police. We made our intentions very clear, although we didn't really mean to carry them out.'

'Then they were hardly intentions. I have heard rumours of a ghostly visitant to some of the flats before Miss Minnie's death. Was this another manifestation of Miss Nutley's nocturnal wanderings?'

'I shouldn't think so,' said Hempseed. 'Niobe's in-and-out-the-windows all happened after Chelion's arrest, and were caused by that.'

'So you didn't have any night visitor while Miss Minnie was alive?'

'No, *we* didn't,' replied Hempseed. 'The ghost, so-called, seems to have intruded on Billie and Elysée and on Niobe herself. Otherwise it (or she) merely prowled up and down the stairs. I believe one or two people swore it had come into their rooms, but people will imagine anything when there's a scare on.'

'Was there really a scare?'

The couple exchanged glances and then Cassie said, 'I think two people found the anonymous letters a lot more frightening than the ghost, although I suppose everybody has some skeleton or other in the cupboard.'

'But nobody except the two young women was sufficiently disturbed by the letters to give up living here.'

'Well, it's not all that easy to find a decent place you can rent, and, as I say, people *talked* about getting the letters and that took the sting out of them, of course. And, by the way, I was *not* referring to the girls. Billie was livid, not scared.'

'Do you know where the girls went?'

'No. Niobe wanted to find out and to make a fuss about their going, but I suppose the lawyers told her to drop it.'

'And they left before Miss Minnie was drowned?'

'It doesn't mean they couldn't have sneaked back and drowned her,' said Hempseed. 'Billie Kennett struck me as a girl who was capable of anything if her precious Elysée was threatened.'

'That's an opinion,' said Cassie, 'that only a *man* would hold and it's most unfair.'

(4)

'You heard all that, I expect, George,' said his employer, when the couple had gone.

'Literary ladies and gentlemen seldom lower their voices, madam. I could not help overhearing what was said.'

'Quite. Have you encountered any of the outdoor staff at this place, George?'

'Yes, madam. There is a taciturn but knowledgeable individual who cleans the cars belonging to the establishment and in summer keeps the lawns in order. Other gardeners are employed on a part-time basis, but this man Penworthy is permanent.'

'I wonder whether you could engage him in conversation on the subject of sea-bathing?'

'Readily, madam.'

'So far, you see, it appears that nobody except Mr Piper has used the beach here for swimming, and he only in the summer months.'

'It is not, perhaps, the most attractive of beaches, madam.'

'We are hardly seeing it at its best at this time of year, but even so, I think you are right.'

'Would there be any specific question you want Penworthy to answer, madam?'

'If my far-fetched theory should turn out to be a fact, there will be no need to lead him.'

Two days elapsed before George was able to make a report. When he did, he prefaced it by asking respectfully:

'Had you anything to go on, madam, in forming your theory?'

'Oh, yes, I suppose so,' Dame Beatrice replied. 'The woman had drowned; the body was fully-clothed; death by drowning in sea water had taken place some time previous to the discovery of the body, and the face had been badly disfigured after death. Well, what have you to tell me?'

'Apart from Mr Piper, who swam every day up to about the middle of October, the only person to enquire about bathing from the beach here was a Miss Kennett, but she never actually took to the water. She and a woman friend, it seems, left the house before the murder was discovered.'

'But not, perhaps, before it had been committed, one is left to infer.'

'As to that, I could not say, madam. It seems that Miss Kennett and her friend ran a small car which Penworthy kept tuned up for them. They used it mainly for business purposes, and he got to know both ladies quite well. Miss Kennett asked about bathing from the beach and confided to him that it was (in her expression) mucky, a description with which he agreed, although, he said it was safe enough for swimming.'

'And nobody else swam from the beach?'

'He says not, so far as his knowledge goes, and as he's always about the place tending the lawn and tidying up those high banks behind this bungalow, I think he would know, madam.'

'He did not mention Miss Niobe Nutley?'

'He did, madam, but only to tell me that she did not fancy the beach here, either. Before Mr Piper took up residence, Penworthy says she used to drive once or twice a week to a beautiful clean beach over on the other side of the bay. She used to say she wanted to get away from all the noise and mess while the workmen were doing the repairs and alterations to the house. This, as I understand, was before Mr Piper returned from France. After he came back she never asked to be taken to the seaside at all and she certainly never bathed from the beach here.'

'But that is not all you have to tell me, or you would not have asked me whether I had anything to go on in formulating my theory. There is one other point. I wonder whether they ever get trespassers? At low tide it must be quite easy for people to walk on the sands and find this bit of beach. Still, a complete stranger would hardly have murdered Miss Minnie. What else?'

'In a word, madam, although the beach here was not used by any of the residents except Mr Piper, Miss Minnie was a great believer in sea water baths. It seems she suffered from rheumatism and she believed that hot sea water baths gave her relief.'

'Ah, splendid! So that accounts for the sea water. I take it that this man Penworthy supplied it to the bungalow.'

'Three times a week, for a small emolument, he was commissioned to bring her four buckets of sea water which she used to let stand for a day to let any sand settle and then she boiled three bucketfuls in kettles and a large iron saucepan kept for the purpose, and the other bucketful was used to cool the hot sea water when she had poured it into the bath.'

'How does he know all this?'

'I deemed it better not to enquire, madam.'

'I suppose he took a peep through the kitchen window. I notice it is uncurtained. He could hardly have peered into the bathroom itself, as the window is of frosted glass. Possibly, of course, she described the process to him. She seems to have been a lonely person and may have been glad of someone to talk to. I suppose he didn't murder her himself and make off with her money and valuables?'

'He does not strike me as the type, madam,' replied George gravely.

'I was not entirely serious when I asked the question, George.'

She left the bungalow and, knowing that Constance was out, went to call on Evesham Evans. She found him frying sausages and bacon and apologised for disturbing him.

'That's all right,' said Evesham. 'Make yourself at home. I'm only frying for the need of something to do. Constance has gone up to Town to chivvy her publisher as usual, so, again, I'm on my own. Take a seat if you can find a sitting-room chair that isn't cluttered, and I'll bring this panful along. Any good inviting you to join me? I know it's a bit early in the day, but I've got stuck with my book and can't get on, so I thought I'd cook a bit of lunch while I waited for inspiration.'

Dame Beatrice said that she had been having cocktails and a snack in the bungalow and was hardly ready for her lunch. She asked whether she might come back later.

'Sure, sure. Glad to see you,' said Evesham, relieved, she thought, that he had no need to share his meal with her.

'Come at three. I'll have the place squared up a bit by then. Did you,' he added suddenly, as she reached the door, 'did you call about anything special?'

'Yes,' she replied, 'but it may take a little time. I want to know all that you know about the death of Miss Minnie. Perhaps you would be willing to go over the salient facts in your mind while you are eating your lunch.'

(5)

'Do I take it that you're a relative?' asked Evesham, when she arrived at three.

'No, I am not a relative.' She produced her official card. Evesham put on a pair of horn-rimmed spectacles which, coupled with two tufts of hair which stuck up like two little ears, gave him the appearance of a tolerant and sagacious owl, and studied the morsel of pasteboard. 'Lestrange Bradley? Consultant psychiatrist to the Home Office, eh? So they think young Piper's *non compos*, do they? I wouldn't have thought that, you know. Still, I expect Broadmoor or Rampton, or whatever, is a shade preferable to the ordinary gaol, although personally I'd opt to be incarcerated with the thugs rather than with the loonies. All the same, I wouldn't have thought Piper was either. A very decent, quiet fellow I found him. Not at all the type to resort to violence.'

'Was Miss Minnie the kind of woman to invite violence?'

'I wouldn't have thought that, either, but I hardly knew her. Kept herself very much to herself, you know. Not exactly one of the gang.'

'Do you look upon yourselves as a kind of family unit, then? Do people like to feel that they are members of a party? Was that, for instance, what made *you* choose to come here to live?'

'Constance chose to come here. Suits her work, she says, although why she thinks so, when she's always pinching the car and careering off to London, I can't understand. Personally, I'd much prefer a flat more in the centre of things. Liverpool, now. I'd like to live in Liverpool. I like to be where there's some action. I like noise and ships and docks and hordes of people.'

'But your wife prefers Weston Pipers, and you are chivalrous enough to do as she wishes.'

'Well,' said Evesham, handing back the card and removing his glasses, 'she earns about ten times as much money as I do, so she reckons to call the tune. Not that I'd want to write *her* kind of bilge, mind you. In fact, I doubt whether a man *could* write it.'

'Mr Hempseed seems to do very well with his page on a woman's paper, I believe.'

'Oh, yes, but Polly writes tongue in cheek. He's shown me some of the things he'd *like* to put in. He's no end of a lad when you get him on his own. Not that *that* happens very often. Cassie McHaig keeps him on a very tight rein. I can't think why he puts up with her. I can't understand why he ever teamed up with her in the first place. Damn it all, *she* doesn't hold the purse-strings, and heaven knows she's got nothing in the way of looks or even talent to recommend her. Ask me what I think, and I'd say she caught him young and trained him early and now the poor devil can't call his soul his own and doesn't have the guts to up and leave her.'

'I believe the theological view is that nobody can call his soul his own. We have elsewhere our sphere.'

'Miss Minnie was some sort of hot gospeller, I believe. I went to the inquest. I was present when the body was found, you know. Some elderly bloke in a gown and a flowing white tie had to identify it. He described himself as Leader, I remember, and said that Miss Minnie was – had been – the editor of his – well, I forget what he called it, but it approximated to his parish magazine.'

'It must have had an enormous circulation.'

'How do you make that out?'

'Well,' said Dame Beatrice, glancing around the handsome apartment, 'judging by the rent I pay, these flats are hardly what one might call inexpensive. Of course, Miss Minnie occupied the bungalow. That may make a difference. I pay less for my servant than for myself.'

'I don't know what the others pay, but I know I couldn't afford to live here on my own. I've got a feeling, though, that there must be a scale of charges according to what people can pay. I can't imagine, for example, how a couple of girls like

Billie and Elysée could have managed the rent here and I reckon the same went for Miss Minnie. Targe, I believe, does very well and so does little Shard. Young Irelath Moore is heavily subsidised by his papa in Canada, so he's well-heeled, but the three females, especially poor old Minnie, must have been given a pretty substantial rebate, I would think, to allow them to live on these premises.'

'Perhaps no other prospective tenant wanted to rent the bungalow.'

'So Minnie got it particularly cheap, you mean? Could be, I suppose. It may be damp, being so near the water.'

'When you saw the body – I understand that you, together with Mr Piper and Mr Targe, broke into the bungalow—'

'Yes, at Piper's instigation, we did, and that's a thing I don't understand and that's why I think, dotty or sane, he *could* have done it, hard though I find it to believe. For one thing, being the owner, he must have had a key to the bungalow, you see. What was to stop him opening up and having a look round on his own? Why go to the length of routing out Targe and me to abet him in smashing a window? Only because he knew the body was there and he didn't want to be on his own when he found it, one would think.'

'You are changing your mind about Mr Piper?'

'Well, no, but one has to look on all sides.'

'So, to finish the question I was about to ask, when you saw the body, what were your first thoughts?'

'I didn't have any. I mean, I didn't have any feelings but revulsion and shock. Then Targe beat it back to the house to get to a telephone and left Piper and me on our own. Well, when I had pulled myself together, I realised that Piper couldn't stand being in the room with the body, but, then, neither could I, for the matter of that, so when he suggested that we adjourn to the sitting-room, I thought it was a very sound idea. It was when I spotted this dirty great poker lying on the hearthrug in there that I—'

'Leapt to the conclusion—?'

'Well, you can't help thinking things, can you? After all, the poor old dame's head had been pretty severely battered, so, naturally, when I spotted the poker, it did occur to me to wonder whether I was in company with her murderer.'

'So you picked up the poker?'

'Well, what would *you* have done? I may write tough books, but I am by no means a tough character and I didn't like the wild expression on Piper's face.'

'Don't you think he was suffering from shock, just as you were?'

'That didn't occur to me at the time. I only know that I grabbed up that poker pretty damn quick, so that I was in a position to defend myself if he started anything, but all he said was that we might as well have the electric fire on. That's my point about the poker, you see. Miss M. didn't need one. It must have been brought there by the murderer.'

'But why was she murdered?'

'Oh, that's simple enough. The old girl had been having a lot of fun writing nasty unsigned letters to the people who had flats in the house. Of course I don't suppose anybody really had anything to hide. Writers get to know a lot of things about one another and I'd have heard any scandal that was going.'

'Did you yourself receive one of the letters?'

'Yes, I did.'

'You have not kept it, I suppose?'

'Yes, I have, and I'll show it you if you like.'

'By the way, now that you know why I am here, may I trouble you to respect my alias for the time being? I do not want to cause alarm to a possibly guilty party. Now what about your anonymous letter?'

'Oh, well, it's rather a good specimen of so-called black humour. It says that I live on my wife's immoral earnings. In a sense it's so damn *true* when you know the bilge Constance writes and the sinful amount she gets paid for it. Immoral earnings? Well, they are! And I live on them? Up to a point, I suppose I do!'

'What made you suppose that Mr Piper had a key to the bungalow and could let himself in whenever he chose?'

'Oh, well, he was the landlord, wasn't he?'

'I understood that Miss Nutley was the possessor of a master-key.'

'*Somebody* was. Did you hear about our ghost?'

'It seems that Miss Minnie may have been the intruder.'

'That was Niobe Nutley's idea. Something about a missing

will. If there was such a thing, and Piper knew of it, he might
have wanted the old girl out of the way. The only thing is that
I can't imagine him smashing up her face after he had killed
her. Very nasty, that, you know. Still, if he hasn't got all his
marbles, that might explain it.'

'Black humour?' said Dame Beatrice thoughtfully. 'Not a
perquisite of elderly women, one would have imagined.' And
her thoughts turned to the elfin Mandrake Shard again. He
was a far more likely 'black' humorist than Miss Minnie, she
decided.

CHAPTER 8

Niobe, All Tears

'I have heard some very disturbing news,' said Dame Beatrice, having opened the door of Niobe's office in response to a notice which read: *Please Ring and Enter.*

'Oh, really, Mrs Farintosh? I am sorry to hear that. I hope it does not mean that you want to leave us? Your contract, which I modified greatly, at your request, from our usual three-year agreement, has more than a month to run.'

'Oh, I shall honour it so far as the rent is concerned, of course. The question is whether I can bring myself to stay. I consider that you ought to have informed me before I took up my tenancy.'

'Of what, Mrs Farintosh?'

'That the owner of Weston Pipers, Mr Piper himself, is being remanded in custody under suspicion of having murdered one of the tenants.'

'But I thought that was common knowledge, Mrs Farintosh. It has been in all the papers. Besides, Mr Piper is innocent. Nobody who knows him has the slightest doubt about that.'

'But if he did not do this dreadful thing, that only makes matters worse.'

'How so? – oh, do please sit down.'

'The murderer may still be living here. In that case nobody is safe,' said Dame Beatrice, seating herself and lowering her voice.

'The murderer was a burglar or a tramp. You need have no fear that he is still on the premises,' said Niobe sharply.

'Then why has Mr Piper been arrested?'

'Oh, there were suspicious circumstances, of course, but I am sure they will all be cleared up at the trial. It is the time of waiting that is so trying. I need – I need your sympathy, Mrs

Farintosh, not a threat to leave me. I am having to cope all alone. It is not easy for me, this period of bearing full responsibility. I am accountable to Mr Piper – to Chelion–' her eyes filled with tears – 'while he is in this dreadful predicament. So far, I have been able to prevail upon most of the tenants to stay, and Mr Moore and his – er – his wife have even returned from America – he has been on a lecture tour over there, you know – and are taking up their option on their flat.'

'I have met Mr and Mrs Moore, of course. They are a charming couple.'

'He is the distinguished Canadian-Irish poet.' Niobe wiped her eyes and essayed a smile.

'Is he a descendant of the Thomas Moore who wrote the delightful *Irish Melodies* and was Lord Byron's biographer?'

'I could not say, but I should think it very likely.'

'Did the Moores know that murder was committed here while they were away? It might have affected their willingness to return if they *did* know, don't you think?'

'No, I don't,' said Niobe shortly. 'The burglar or tramp, or whatever, killed that old lady in the bungalow, not in the house. The house is completely protected.'

'Oh, but I was told that the poor woman was drowned in the sea.'

'Oh, well, yes, of course, but the body was found in the bungalow. That is one of the reasons why the police thought –' she sniffed dolorously – 'they thought Chelion had done it. They said that an outsider would have left the body in the sea so that the outgoing tide could carry it away. We have thirty-foot tides here, you see. The water comes almost up to the lawn at high tide and then goes out ever so far.'

'So I have noticed. You have not resolved my apprehensions. The house itself may be burglar-proof, but that is beside the point. One does not spend the whole of one's time behind a locked door. You not only omitted to tell me that Mr Piper is a suspected murderer; you even allowed me to rent the bungalow for my manservant.'

'You suggested it yourself! It was for your own convenience that you housed him in the bungalow. Good heavens,' cried

Niobe, beginning to weep again, 'if every house which has had a dead body in it were never to be lived in again, more than half the population would be homeless!'

'A dead body is one thing, Miss Nutley. A murdered body is quite another. You should have told me.' (I am being completely unscrupulous, thought Dame Beatrice, but murder is not a thing to be too nice about.)

'Well, I'm sure I'm very sorry you were not told, but I have a responsibility to Mr Piper – to Chelion – while this wretched time goes on. If everybody thought as you do, he would be coming back to an empty house, his livelihood gone.' Niobe began to weep again.

'Oh, the rents are his livelihood, are they? I was given to understand that he was a wealthy man in his own right,' said the unsympathetic listener.

'I don't know who told you so, but, be that as it may, I am still responsible for the lettings,' snapped Niobe, dabbing at her eyes. 'Besides, that wretched dead woman was attempting to claim the property.'

'It is interesting that all the tenants are writers. Is that merely a coincidence or is it an idiosyncrasy of Mr Piper's?' asked Dame Beatrice, on a different note.

'As a matter of fact,' said Niobe, who appeared to be relieved by the apparent change of subject, 'I selected the tenants myself. Chelion had nothing to do with choosing them. He is an embryo author himself, you see, so I thought he would like to be surrounded by his own kind.'

'An *embryo* author?'

'By that I mean so far he has not had anything published.'

'It must be very frustrating to get what I believe are called pink slips.'

'That hasn't happened – yet. Chelion is still working on his first novel.'

'Oh, I see. So, to encourage him, you filled his house with other writers.'

'All of whom are successful in their own sphere. Psychologically a very sound idea, don't you think? I mean, you ought to know. You represented yourself in your letter as a contributor to psychiatric journals.'

'Talking of letters, Miss Nutley, one or two of my fellow-tenants have referred to some unpleasant, unsigned missives which people here have received from time to time.'

'Poor old Miss Minnie wrote them,' said Niobe in a positive tone.

'Can you be sure of that?'

'Well, no more have been written since she died. Proof positive, I should say.'

'Hardly proof positive, I would have thought. Did Mr Piper receive one?'

'I don't know. He has never said so.' (Lie number one, thought Dame Beatrice.)

'You yourself—?'

'Oh, yes, I got one. I've destroyed it, of course.'

'Oh, of course. Such pernicious things are apt to contain a grain of truth, are they not? In that case, to destroy them is the only possible course if one wants to restore one's peace of mind.'

'Mine did not contain any truth.' Tears came into her eyes again. (How prophetic were her parents at her baptism! Or can it be that it pleases her to live up to her name? thought Dame Beatrice.) 'It accused me of being Chelion's mistress,' Niobe went on, attempting a watery smile

'Oh, dear! How very annoying for you.'

'We were engaged to be married before he came into money, but of course I released him when I realised how wealthy he was. There has been nothing between us since. As soon as I knew what had happened I offerred him his freedom and he took it and went off to Paris.' Here she broke down completely, put her head on the writing-table at which she was sitting and sobbed aloud. Dame Beatrice pursed up her beaky little mouth and waited until the paroxysm was over. Then she said:

'I will not play cat and mouse with you any longer. I am here on official business. One of your tenants recognised me and, so far, has kept his own counsel. Another I have confided in. Now I feel it is your turn.'

Niobe, tear-stained, swollen-eyed and unattractively blotched, raised her head.

'My turn for what?' she asked.

'To be put in the picture. As a psychiatrist – oh, yes, that is true enough – I entertain certain doubts about the wisdom of the county police in having arrested and charged Mr Piper, so I have decided to look into the case on behalf of the Home Office.'

'But Chelion doesn't plead – what do they call it? – diminished responsibility, does he?' asked Niobe, staring at her visitor out of red-rimmed eyes.

'No. He claims that he is completely innocent of the charge and I am inclined – I go no further than that – I am *inclined* to believe him now that I have his own account of the matter.'

There was no doubt that Niobe was able to recover quickly from her bouts of weeping. She looked alert, wary and interested.

'Well, this is somewhat of a surprise and I find it rather disconcerting,' she said. 'I had no idea that he was in need of a psychiatrist, especially of one who is employed to visit prisons.'

This statement was made in so venomous a tone that it seemed she thought it best to qualify it by saying, 'One feels so helpless when one comes up against the police and the law.'

'I suppose so, yes. Most unfortunately there is a very strong piece of evidence against him which cannot be ignored or glossed over.'

'I suppose you refer to the fact that Miss Minnie may have had claims upon Mrs Dupont-Jacobson's fortune,' said Niobe, nodding soberly and then shaking her head.

'Exactly. It makes the case against him look very dark.'

'I know.' Niobe's eyes filled with tears again, but this time she did not break down. 'And, of course,' she added, 'she was drowned in the sea, and Chelion was the only one of us who ever used this little beach for bathing.'

'Yes,' said Dame Beatrice, not choosing at this stage to mention Miss Minnie's sea-water baths and curious to know whether Niobe would do so. If she did not, it could be that she did not know of them, but the gardener, after all, was her servant and no doubt she would have kept an eye on his activities. There was a long pause. Dame Beatrice saw it as a deliberate attempt on Niobe's part to force her to make the next move. She decided to make it. 'Yes,' she said again. 'I wonder at what time of day or night Miss Minnie was drowned?'

'Day – or night? Well, it must have been at night, mustn't it?'

'Why so?'

'Well, I mean – well, if it had been done in daylight, surely some of us would have known about it'

'Will you explain that, please?'

'I should have thought it was obvious. Most of the windows in the sitting-rooms of these flats look out on the park and the lake, of course, but there are some from which the lawn, the bungalow and the beach are visible. Miss Minnie was fully dressed, I understand, when the body was found. Somebody, surely, would have seen her entering the sea if she had done so by daylight.'

'Entering the sea? Voluntarily, you mean?'

'Well, hardly, considering the battering of her head, poor thing. But surely, as it must have been murder, somebody would have heard her protesting, perhaps screaming, or would even have seen her dragged towards the beach.'

'Her protests and her screams could equally well have been heard in the dark, could they not?' (So the possibility of sea water baths taken inside the bungalow was not going to be mentioned, thought Dame Beatrice. Perhaps, though, after all, Niobe knew nothing of the buckets of sea water scooped up by Penworthy and peddled by him to the rheumatic old lady; or perhaps she had so much guilty knowledge of them that she was not prepared to mention them.)

Dame Beatrice did not wait for an answer to her question, but continued: 'At what time did Miss Minnie retire for the night?'

'Oh, all sorts of times. I have seen her light go off at nine and I have known it to be still on at two in the morning.' (So you kept a watch on the bungalow, thought Dame Beatrice.)

'I have been told that you suspected her of breaking into this house at night,' she said.

'Yes. There were complaints, so I had all the downstair windows made secure, as well as the doors.'

'Very wise. But why, Miss Nutley –' here Dame Beatrice made her own dramatic pause – 'why do you follow her example?'

'What do you mean? My rooms are in the house by right. I do not need to break in!'

'Not into the house, but into some of the tenants' rooms.'

'I have *never* done such a thing! Well, not deliberately. Who told you that I had? I suppose somebody has shown you one of those abominable letters! As a matter of fact, there you have the grain of truth you yourself mentioned. I *did* inadvertently enter a room that was not my own. I mistook it for Chelion's, that is all. I went to look over his clothes to see whether there was mending to be done or anything to be sent to the cleaners.'

'A strange mistake, surely, since Mr Piper's rooms were on the ground floor and the room I am told you entered was upstairs.'

'I was confused. I hardly knew what I was doing. You have no idea of the shock I had when poor Chelion was arrested.'

'Yes, shock can have strange effects. What caused two of your tenants to leave Weston Pipers?'

Niobe did not appear surprised by the change of subject.

'Billie Kennett and Elysée Barnes?' she said. 'I think they found the rent a little above their means. I had to let them go, although their lease had quite a long time to run.'

'They were not the victims of persecution, by any chance?'

'Persecution? What do you mean?'

'Were they happy together?'

'So far as I know.'

'Sometimes, Miss Nutley, an unhappily married woman can become extremely envious of the happily unmarried, especially those of her own sex. I have known cases.'

'Some people would rather be unhappily married than not married at all.'

'That also is true. Is it certain that Miss Minnie had no attachments?'

'So far as I know, she had none, except that elderly man who attended the inquest, but he could hardly be called an attachment.'

'Why do you say that?'

'He was merely the head of that religious sect for which, I believe, she edited some sort of magazine.'

'How do you think the murderer actually drowned his victim?'

'I would rather not speculate. It is a horrid subject for thought, just simply horrible.'

'As the body was fully clothed, she could hardly have been drowned in the bath.'

'Of course not. She was drowned in the sea. He overpowered her – she was elderly and frail – and plunged her in.'

'I still think it was a very stupid murder. If it happened as you suggest – and of course you realise that the suggestion implicates Mr Piper, as it did when you made it to the police – why on earth was not the body left in the sea? – a point we have already touched on. In that case, don't you see, it would have been so easy to make it look like suicide. It would have been worth the risk, for in the case of anybody known to be somewhat eccentric, suicide would have been taken for granted.'

'The murderer must have had a reason,' said Niobe, 'but we shall never know what it was.'

'Oh, yes, we shall, Miss Nutley. The murder had to look like murder. A verdict of suicide would not have suited the murderer's plans at all.'

'That does not make sense to me.'

'What other explanation can you offer?'

'Explanations of other people's dreadful deeds are beyond me. And now, Mrs Farintosh, I am a very busy person.'

'Of course. I thought you might like to know that there may be help at hand for Mr Piper.'

'Help? Just to get him into Broadmoor instead of Dartmoor? A distinction without a difference!'

'Ah, well, we shall see. My researches are beginning to make certain matters clearer. Oh, one other thing: did Miss Minnie ever have visitors?'

'Not to my knowledge.'

'Not even at night?'

Niobe changed colour. She looked both angry and frightened.

'Have you been questioning my tenants?' she demanded.

'Certainly.'

'Then I must ask you to go. Enough mud has been stirred up already.'

'And enough sea-sand, too. I understand that grains of it were found in the nasal passages, around the dentures and under the tongue of the corpse.'

'Your remarks are revolting!'

'The truth often is. I could cite you many instances.'

'Please go. You frighten me. Leave my house and take your manservant – if *that's* what he is – with you.'

'Well, he is not a plain-clothes police officer,' said Dame Beatrice, 'although I think that is hardly what you inferred.' She cackled with real mirth. 'Well, Miss Nutley, I understand your feelings. I still think it was a stupid crime. If a verdict of suicide would not have fitted in with the murderer's plans, would it not have been much simpler to have murdered her inside the bungalow and left the body there? Obviously the murderer knew how to get in. That is why I asked about visitors.'

'Now that I come to remember,' said Niobe reluctantly, 'I believe you have hit on the explanation. I found my gardener carrying buckets of sea water up to the bungalow door. He said they were for Miss Minnie's sea water baths.'

'Ah, that would explain everything,' said Dame Beatrice in a tone of deep satisfaction. 'But had you never thought of it before?'

'Never. I have been so confused and so upset that my normal faculties simply have not been functioning. Well, I am set on your leaving us, but I had no intention of deceiving you. I thought everybody knew about Chelion's arrest and the awful accusation against him, yet you say you did not know. Now you admit—'

'I did not say I did not know. I said you should have told me when you let me the rooms, and particularly when you let me the bungalow for my manservant.'

'That is not the way to do business, and, if you knew, you knew, so there is no need to reproach me. Had I realised that you were connected with the police—'

'With the Home Office.'

'What is the difference? If I had known what you were, I would never have let to you at all. I am the one who was deceived.'

'So I am rejected and ejected and, withal, not without a stain on my character,' said Dame Beatrice to Laura, giving her a ferocious grin.

'How come? Though I'm glad to have you back.'

Dame Beatrice gave the substance of her conversation with Niobe.

'Well, I should think you'd expect her to chuck you out after you had led her up the garden with all that rot about how she ought to have told you about the murder, and then let her know that you'd known about it all along.'

'True. If I were able to feel contrition I should feel it now. Incidentally, she had already turned me out before we reached the last stages.'

'But I suppose there was method in your madness, as usual. Did you *want* to get slung out?'

'Sometimes summary dismissal is preferable to a long-drawn-out departure accompanied by tears.'

'Oh, Lord! She is Niobe both by name and nature, eh? So what's the next job? Those two girls who, so your letters inform me, have fled the joint, I suppose.'

'How right you always are! Yes, indeed. They are now the only pebbles left on my beach.'

'Oh, well, you won't need to stub your toe on them, then. Do you know where to find them?'

'I traced Miss Kennett through the newspaper she works for. I sent a letter to her in care of the editor, he passed it on and I have had an answer from her with her new address. She has invited me to call on Sunday and where she is we shall also find Miss Barnes, no doubt.'

This did not turn out to be the case. Billie herself opened the front door to them.

'Oh, yes,' she said, 'Dame Beatrice, isn't it? And Mrs Gavin? Oh, yes, do come in. Sorry Elysée isn't here. I believe you wanted to see both of us.'

CHAPTER 9

Billie and the Witch

'I expect you yourself can tell me anything I need to know,' said Dame Beatrice, when the three of them were seated in a tiny room which overlooked a scrap of green hardly large enough to be called a lawn, 'unless you would prefer to wait until Miss Barnes comes in.'

'She won't,' said Billie, her square face firmly set and her eyes full of misery. 'She's left me. She went off yesterday with a man.'

'Would you rather I came back another day, I wonder?'

'No, it wouldn't make any difference. It's about this business at The Vipers, I think you said. Don't know that I can tell you much about it. We got out before any of it happened.'

'So I understand.'

'Anonymous letters, you know. Why should anybody bother to throw filth about? We had no enemies. We did nobody any harm.'

'I am surprised that in these days you paid any attention to the letters.'

'*I* wouldn't have done. It was Elysée who couldn't take what they dished out. I know why, now, of course. She was afraid of losing this bloke she's gone off with. She must have thought he'd opt out if the facts of our – well, our friendship – came his way.'

'Did you know, while you were living at Weston Pipers, that this man existed?

'Yes, and I've always been prepared. What's *your* connection with Weston Pipers, anyway? What's the Home Office got to do with Chelion Piper?'

'Well, nobody wants a miscarriage of justice, surely?'

'Personally, I couldn't care less. I don't suppose there's such a thing as justice in this world and, as I don't believe in the next one, it goes for that, too.'

'I was referring to the law. It has its own interpretation of the word. From what you saw of Mr Piper during your stay at the mansion, what opinion did you form concerning his character?'

'Ah,' said Billie, her sombre expression settling into easier lines, 'now that's a question I *can* answer. I've thought about him a lot since he was arrested, and I feel perfectly certain he didn't drown that old woman. My job is reporting crime, so I tag along to all the big trials. There's always a public for details of murder, rape, arson and so forth. Same public as screams its stupid head off at dirty little jokes and sexy innuendo, I dare say. How I loathe and despise it!'

'So you have attended several trials for murder,' said Dame Beatrice, stemming the flow before it could develop into what she suspected might become a torrent.

'That's what I'm saying. I've seen a number of murderers in the dock and this Piper ought not to be one of them.'

'Can you produce chapter and verse?'

'No. One gets an impression, that's all. Actually I had very little to do with him. All the business dealings were with the bitch.'

'With Miss Nutley?'

'Yes, if you prefer to call her that. My other name for her is Nut Case.'

'Really? A play upon her surname?'

'More of a play upon her nature. I called her a bitch just now, but not in the sense that most women call other women bitches. Niobe Nutley was a cringing, whining, please-don't-kick-me little whelpess who'd attached herself to Piper in the most sickening way you can imagine. Of course, you never saw them together, did you?'

'No, I had not that affecting experience. My impression of Miss Nutley was of a hard-headed businesswoman with unexpectedly sensitive tear-ducts.'

Billie's heavy, sardonic expression had vanished. She lifted her head and laughed aloud in an unaffected shout of amusement.

'I say,' she said, 'would you mind if I used that at some time? It's rather good.'

'I resign the copyright to you.'

'Unexpectedly sensitive tear-ducts! Yes, they're so very sensitive that one suspects the tears may be of the crocodile variety. I mean, it was because of what *she* told the police that Piper got arrested.'

'If you were not there at the time, how do you know that?'

'Through my job. I wasn't sent along to cover the case, but I knew the chap on our paper who got the assignment. Niobe seems to have spread herself on the subject of sea bathing and Minnie's expectations under Chelion's patroness's will.'

'Did you see anything of Miss Minnie while you were at Weston Pipers?'

'No. She was an unsociable old pussy-cat and didn't mix with the sinful likes of us. Elysée used to say she was sorry for her, but my view is that you choose your own way of life and, if you aren't cut out to be a mixer, why try to mix? In a way I envied the old girl her independence. It's not much fun, really and truly, being a slave to another person, whether it's lover, husband, elderly invalid, or widower father. I've experienced most of all that in my time – except the husband angle, of course.'

'You must have a strong protective instinct and a very large heart.'

'Protective instinct, yes, I believe I have. Large heart – well, not that you'd notice. I've hated most of the people I've had to protect.'

'Do you think Miss Nutley has ever felt protective towards Mr Piper?'

'Lord, no! Do you? After all, it seems to have been mostly her evidence which landed him in the soup.'

'As you pointed out, I have never seen them together, so I cannot express an opinion.'

'If you ask me, I sum her up as a woman wailing for her demon lover, and when she can't get him she'd just as soon see him in hell.'

'Or in the condemned hold?'

'Yes, if you like,' said Billie, giving Dame Beatrice a very straight glance. Dame Beatrice paid it the compliment of asking a direct personal question.

'Are you perhaps attributing to Miss Nutley sentiments which may apply in your own case?'

'No,' said Billie, without showing the slightest sign either of surprise or resentment. 'There are two kinds of love. Mine's the second kind. Men do make passes at Elysée, but I've never really minded until now.'

'Do you know the man who has eloped with Miss Barnes?'

'Yes, and if I met him down a dark alley I'd stick a knife in his ribs.'

'That contradicts your previous assertion, surely?'

'I don't think so. If I believed Elysée would be happy with him, I'd give them my blessing; but she won't be happy with him. He's a rat.'

'Oh, really? That still seems to me a little like wishful thinking.'

'I expect you've met him if you've been staying at the Vipers,' said Billie, ignoring this sally. 'He's Cassie McHaig's stand-off half, Polly Hempseed. I knew he made passes at Elysée, but I never really thought he'd be the one she'd fall for. I believe he's only run off with her to score off Cassie. Mistress McHaig is quite a good sort, but kind of heavy in the hand, I'd say. They were always rowing. *He* thought Cassie was bossy and narrow-minded (which she is) and *she* despised the way he made his money. So do I, in a way, but we poor journalists have to live, I suppose, although there doesn't always seem much point in it.'

'He wrote his Woman's Page with tongue in cheek, I was told. Perhaps that softens the evidence against him.'

'I think it makes him even more of a heel.'

'Did you know that Miss Minnie took hot sea-water baths?' asked Dame Beatrice.

'Oh,' said Billie, 'so *that's* how it was done!'

'It seems a likely theory. I have presented the police with it.'

'But, if they accept it, isn't that enough to clear Piper? I mean, if she was drowned in her own sea water, Piper is no more suspect than anybody else, is he?'

'That is what I have attempted to convey to the authorities.'

'Bully for you! I mean, it's so much more *likely*, isn't it, than that she was dragged out of the bungalow down to the beach and held under water and then her body taken back to her bedroom and coshed. The coshing is the hardest part to understand. I mean, anybody can be excused for committing murder if they have reason enough, but a gratuitous assault on a dead body doesn't seem like the action of a sane person, does it?'

'In my book, as Laura here would put it, no murderer is a sane person, Miss Kennett.'

'That's too sweeping altogether, Dame Beatrice. Surely there might be the best of reasons why certain people should not go on living.'

'Those people would not be murdered; they would be executed.'

'The result would be the same. I think you're splitting hairs.'

'So long as I do not split heads, I am still on the right side of the law. If Mr Hempseed is as unworthy as you think him to be, what was his attraction for your friend?'

'Well, just that she wanted a man, I suppose. Besides, she and I had begun to get on each other's wick a bit. It works that way sometimes in friendships such as ours. It would have settled itself in time, but Elysée didn't give it a chance. All the same, although I'm as sick as mud with her, I'd have her back tomorrow if she'd come, and there would be no recriminations, either. My firm belief is that people can't help what they do. We're all conditioned to make certain mistakes, and we make them. I think Elysée is the most sickening little ass to have fallen for this lonely hearts adjuster, but time will show.'

'It seemed to me,' said Dame Beatrice, 'that only two people at Weston Pipers were what I (possibly in my ignorance) would call happy.'

'You mean Irelath and little Sumatra, don't you? Yes, I'm sure you're right. Niobe is as miserable as sin, poor cow, Polly has gone off with Elysée because he was always at loggerheads with Cassie, who must be feeling suicidal at his defection, and, of course, long ago, I should guess, the Evans couple became fed up with each other, but can't quite face up to a divorce. I'll tell you something else, but it's not for publication. If I had to pick the most likely murderer from among the Viperites, I'd plump for Mandrake Shard every time.'

'His height and his physique might be against him, don't you think?'

'Oh, I think not. He's probably very wiry and tough, in spite of his size, and Minnie was an old lady and probably frail.'

'I do not see him as a violent character, although in his capacity as blackmailer and anonymous letter-writer he is far from harmless.'

'Blackmailer?' Billie had changed colour. 'How did you get on to that? He tried it on us, you know – on Elysée and me – and, in the end, of course, it got her down and she pestered me to agree that we'd leave and find somewhere else to live.'

'Ah, yes,' said Dame Beatrice, 'I was under the impression that you left Weston Pipers because of an anonymous letter. I have the best of reasons for believing that I know who wrote it, but it was not Mr Shard that time.'

'It wasn't?'

'No.'

'How do you know it wasn't?'

'Because the author of it confessed to being the writer.'

'Any use to ask who it was?'

'No.'

'Well, did this person write the other letters as well?'

'I think not. I think the letter you received was – and will be – the only one to emanate from this particular source.'

'Oh,' said Billie, 'I suppose it was that poisonous cat Constance Kent, then. She tried to give me a heart-to-heart once, but I soon showed her the door – with a carving-knife in my hand, I don't mind admitting. I could soon have sorted her out, anyway. It didn't need threats. I knew she had had an illegit. kid and murdered it.'

'Mrs Evans?'

'None other. I covered the case, so I know. Of course she didn't know *me*, but I recognised *her* as soon as I met her at Vipers. It was a local case and I was only a cub reporter at the time. It was before she married Evesham, of course. They've only been married about five years. She got off on the score of diminished responsibility and, anyway, they didn't really prove that it was a wilful act, so the beaks took the broad, charitable view. She changed her name to the one she uses for her books, but I always thought it was an odd thing to pick as her pseudonym the name of another child-murderess.'

'There are doubts about the first Constance Kent.'

'Oh, well, let it go. Is there anything else I can do for you?'

'Only one thing – and you may not be willing to do it.'

'You mean I haven't been of any help, so far, but if I find out where Polly and Elysée are living, you'd like the address. Very well. My personal feelings are of much less importance than that Piper should be cleared. I don't hold much of a brief for men – I've worked with them too long to have many illusions about them – but Piper's all right and he is certainly no murderer of old ladies.'

'Did you know that, among all the inhabitants of Weston Pipers, your friend Miss Barnes probably knew Miss Minnie best?'

'Elysée?'

'Yes. I understand that, when she had the use of your car, she was accustomed to giving Miss Minnie a lift into the town.'

'First I've heard of it.'

'Would you have objected?'

'Of course not. Elysée knew that, or she would have mentioned it.'

'May I ask a question which, without your permission, I have no right to ask?'

'If you're going to ask about my relationship with Elysée—'

'Oh, gracious me, no! It is only those relationships which lead to crime that concern me.'

'Love is love,' said Billie, tritely and unanswerably. 'You don't go in search of it. It finds you, and, when it does, you've had it – in both senses. Never mind that. What's your question?'

'I will put it bluntly. Did you leave Weston Pipers because you could not pay the rent, and *not* because of anonymous letters?'

'No. We shared it fifty-fifty, like the housekeeping and holidays. We managed all right. Has anybody suggested we left in arrears?'

'No, nothing of that sort.'

'Then why did you ask?'

'To clear up a small point.'.

'Of course,' said Billie, 'there was a scale of charges, you know. Our rent was a good deal less than the first-floor people paid. I say, I rather wish Elysée had just mentioned that she was in the habit of giving Miss Minnie a lift in the car. Seems funny that she didn't tell me, now I come to think of it. We always told each other everything.'

'So often a disastrous policy. In any case, I take it that Miss Barnes did not tell you that she intended to elope.'

'Only at the very last minute, but, as I told you, I wasn't all that much surprised. The only surprise I felt was that I couldn't understand her choosing Polly Hempseed.'

'Perhaps there *was* no choice.'

'You don't mean that in quite the way it sounds,' said Billie shrewdly. 'What's the *double entendre?*'

'Not that, exactly. Miss Minnie seems to have been a woman of mystery so far as Weston Pipers was concerned. Can anything have passed between her and Miss Barnes which led to Miss Barnes's going away with Mr Hempseed?'

'Sounds very far-fetched to me.'

'I attach significance to it for one reason only; that Miss Barnes made no mention to you of giving Miss Minnie the lifts, yet Mr Piper, by his own admission, knew of them.'

'Well, he was at home, while I was at work. Elysée only had the car two or three days a week, anyway, and I don't suppose Miss Minnie went shopping every one of those days. I don't think there's anything much in what you're saying.'

'Did Miss Barnes ever go out in the evenings?'

'Without me, you mean? Chelion took her to the pictures once or twice in the town, but otherwise the only times she was out in the evenings was if she had a late modelling session. That happened quite a number of times while we were at Pipers.'

'Not a bad scout, that slightly uncouth and very unhappy blighter,' said Laura, when they had left the house. 'Anyway, for both their sakes I hope she never does meet this Hempseed down a dark alley.'

'She would hardly be likely to have a carving-knife with her.'

'That was an interesting sidelight on Mrs Constance Kent, wasn't it? Do you believe the story?'

'Yes. I had personal experience of the case and an expert opinion was called for.'

'You mean you actually talked to Constance Kent Evans? But that means she must have recognised you when you turned up at Weston Pipers.'

'Oh, I think she did, but she was no more than a girl when the case came up and I expect she hoped that her appearance had sufficiently changed for *me* not to recognise *her*.'

'A bit thick that she should moralise about those two harmless girls when her own slate was hardly what you'd call clean.'

'Oh, guilty people often attempt to blacken others in order to shed some of the load.'

'So, in your opinion, she *did* deliberately murder the baby?'

'Opinion is not fact. Let us abandon the subject. I shall be glad to learn Miss Barnes's new address.'

'You think she'll get in contact with Miss Kennett and let her know where she is?'

'I think Miss Kennett believes that she will, and she is in a better position to judge than we are. Besides, she may well be right in her estimation of Mr Hempseed's character and motives. She is deeply hurt at the moment, but her work has probably made her a pretty good judge of people and particularly of men, since the courts cater, in all respects, much more for that sex than for women.'

'Was she of any help to you? She seemed to think she wasn't.'

'She took kindly to the theory that Miss Minnie was drowned in sea water but not in *open* water.'

'What does that prove?'

'Nothing.'

'There's only one thing against the theory, you know.'

'Yes, I do know and I have given thought to it. You mean that if Miss Minnie was drowned while she was taking a bath, the body would hardly have been found fully clothed.'

'Or on the bed, come to that.'

'As I say, I have given thought to these things and have attempted to make a reconstruction of what must have happened. I do not believe that Miss Minnie was drowned either in the sea or in her bath. The buckets of sea water were left to settle, so that any sand might fall to the bottom of the pail. The murderer had only to watch the pails being delivered to the bungalow by Penworthy to know that the means of drowning Miss Minnie were to hand and would remain so for several hours.'

'You mean he simply broke in and held her head down in one of the buckets?'

'And then carried the body, which would have been fully clothed, into the bedroom and laid it on the bed while he (or she, of course) spied out the lie of the land. The plan, I am sure, was then to have transported the body to the beach and put it into the water to indicate suicide. I hold this opinion despite the discussion I had with Niobe Nutley.'

'Then why on earth wasn't that done? If it had been, a charge of murder would never have been brought and poor old Minnie would still have been got out of the way.'

'Dear me,' said Dame Beatrice, 'the whole point was not only to get Miss Minnie out of the way, but to involve Mr Piper. Almost at the last moment, I think, the murderer saw his (or her) error. A suicide would never do. It still had to look like what it was – murder. There was probably a moment of indecision; almost, if not quite, a moment of panic. Then, as a last resort, I think the murderer took up the remaining buckets of sea water and soused the whole of the body (and, of course, the bed) with them.'

'And the poker-work, or whatever, on the head?'

'Frustration, because what had seemed a perfect plan had, at the last minute, miscarried, perhaps, but there is a more likely explanation.'

'Such as?'

'Work it out for yourself. It is very simple.'

'Well, it wasn't Piper's and it can hardly have been Niobe Nutley's plan.'

'Why not? I agree that a swimming instructor, man or woman, would be the last person (owing to the inhibitions induced by his or her training) to drown another in open water, but he or she probably would not be averse to drowning puppies or kittens in a bucket.'

'You make me feel quite ill,' said Laura. 'So, if it wasn't Piper, it was Niobe.'

'Not necessarily, of course. One must keep an open mind.'

'The reason for bashing the face of the corpse? To cover up other facial injuries, I suppose.'

woman who took up residence in the bungalow. The three men who broke in and found the body were in no doubt that it was that of the woman they knew as Miss Minnie.'

'But they seem to have seen very little of her while she was alive, and to some people who are not particularly interested or not very observant, I dare say one old lady they haven't seen much of looks very like other old ladies of about the same age and size.'

'There is, as always, much in what you say. I can readily obtain the pastor's address from the police, so let us pay him a visit.'

The pastor proved to be a plump, smooth-faced, smiling individual whom Laura immediately wrote off as a scoundrel. Dame Beatrice, more perceptively, recognised that he was an Eurasian, probably half-Sinhalese, half-English. The address she had been given was that of a murky little junk shop in a side street of the seaside town nearest to Weston Pipers. The side street, which was partly cobbled roadway, partly widely-spaced steps, went steeply uphill from the seaside promenade which was the high street of the pleasant, unpretentious little town, and the shop was on a corner where the cobbled road ended and the flight of steps began.

It had two windows, one on to the cobbled street, the other on to a narrow concreted way which ran parallel with the high street. Dame Beatrice studied both windows of the shop before she entered. One was cluttered with items which included such miscellaneous objects as a bicycle pump, two dejected-looking, grimy, pink parasols, a torn lace fan, a rolled-up pair of unsavoury-looking corsets, a set of heavy steel fire-irons, a pair of oleographs depicting rural scenes, and there were also half a dozen vases of various sizes, shapes and colours arranged around a couple of pitchers of the kind used as part of the furniture of an old-fashioned wash-hand stand.

The other window displayed, among less identifiable objects, several wine glasses, a decanter which had lost its glass stopper, some china trinket-boxes, a Malay kris and a Balkan yataghan.

'Well,' said Dame Beatrice, 'we had better steel ourselves to make a purchase. Has your fancy strayed in favour of any of these, to my mind, undesirable objects?'

'Wonder how much they want for that thing in the leather-covered scabbard? Hamish collects swords and I don't think he's got one of that type.'

'The yataghan? It will make an excellent bargaining-point. If it is as good a specimen as it looks, the blade will be damascened.'

The proprietor, whom they had noticed taking stock of them from behind a lace curtain, came forward as soon as they entered and made them an ingratiating bow.

'You have seen something you like, ladies?'

'Perhaps we may look around,' said Dame Beatrice, noting that *objects d'art* littered three small tables in the middle of the shop.

'But of course! Take your time. A pleasant day, is it not? You are visitors to the town, perhaps?'

Without answering, except with a reptilian smile which made the fat proprietor banish his own in favour of a grave inclination of the head and a hastily-sketched gesture designed to counteract the Evil Eye, Dame Beatrice picked up and studied one or two repellent pieces of china and glass and a paper-knife in the form of a fish, asked the price of each, shook her head as though in regret that the amount was beyond her means and then asked:

'Does your stock contain anything from the house which is now called Weston Pipers? I believe most of the furniture and effects were sold when the previous owner died.'

'You have a connection with the house, madam?'

'As a temporary tenant, yes. A very dreadful affair, the murder which, I am told, took place there recently, but I believe the police have made an arrest.' She walked over to the torn lace curtain which only partly screened the collection of which the yataghan formed an item, as though to indicate that she had no further interest in the murder. She peered at the sorry display in the window. The proprietor came and stood at her shoulder.

'The only things I have from the house,' he said, in a purring tone which brought the suspicious Laura level with him, a heavy glass paperweight in her hand, 'are a fine set of fire-irons. With all this central heating and electric fires of the present day, there is little call for such things. If madam would care to have a memento of Weston Pipers I would accept a cheap price.'

'I have seen something in your shop I like better. I wonder whether *that* came from Weston Pipers as well?'

'I think not, madam, but please to point it out.'

Dame Beatrice turned and faced that side of the room where the wall was partly barred off by a small wooden counter which held a till. On the wall, its only ornament, was a strange little picture hardly visible in the dim light of the interior of the shop.

It depicted a head with three aspects. One was full-face, the other two were in profile. On the top of the head was an erection which looked like a broad-based, rather sqat vase and surrounding this were the two horns of the crescent moon. The head was one of dignified, disdainful malignity. It had broad, negroid features and a thick, curved, sensual, cruel mouth. The eyes were set unnaturally high on the fore-head, the creature had no ears. Dame Beatrice pointed to it.

'At my own home I have a little niche where that would go,' she said. 'How much are you asking for it?'

'Oh, that is not for sale, I'm afraid, madam.'

'A pity. I have a taste for the grotesque. Is it a talisman of some kind? Your good luck sign, perhaps?'

'Nothing of the sort. Is there anything else you have seen?'

Laura, who had begun to think that she was not to be allowed to make an offer for the yataghan, cut in on him to ask:

'What do you want for that sword-thing in the window?'

Obviously relieved to have someone other than Dame Beatrice to deal with, the bland proprietor drew aside the curtain, took up the yataghan and handed it over.

'A very nice piece,' he said. 'A duelling sword of best French workmanship of the eighteenth century. Beautiful all-leather sheath.'

Laura drew the weapon out of its scabbard. The blade, although tarnished, was not rusty, and it was damascened in silver whorls and twirls.

Dame Beatrice took sword and scabbard from Laura and looked them over.

'A battle sword of Balkan manufacture,' she said. 'Nine-teenth, not eighteenth, century. The scabbard is of wood covered thinly with leather. Name your price.'

'I am a very poor man, as you can see, madam. As for the sword, I knew what it was, of course, but people are more impressed by an earlier century of workmanship. I did not expect to come up against an expert in a place like this.' He pouted childishly and looked away.

'Dishonesty is *not* the best policy,' said Laura sternly. 'Well, how much?'

The proprietor glanced at Dame Beatrice and then at Laura.

'It is a nice piece,' he said hesitantly. 'Would ten pounds interest you?'

'Done!' said Laura, opening her handbag.

'Well, well!' said Dame Beatrice. 'The collector's acumen appears to be missing from your make-up! You should not have been so precipitate.'

The proprietor twisted his hands together.

'The lady has made an agreement!' he said, in agony. 'Look, I'll throw in the fire-irons for you yourself if you do not dispute with me. You shall have the fire irons for nothing!'

'But not the little picture I fancy so much?'

'I cannot part with it. It has religious significance. Please accept the fire-irons. They are very nice.'

'Do you hold services here, then?'

'Oh, well, as to that—' He turned away from both of them and put Laura's notes into the till. Then he rummaged around to find wrappings for the fire-irons and the yataghan. At last he handed over the packages and, bowing and smiling, opened the shop door, saw them out and would have followed them to their car but that the stolid chauffeur was already holding the car door open for them.

'Did I get stung over the yataghan?' asked Laura, when they were seated and George had reversed the car.

Dame Beatrice cackled. 'I hardly think so,' she said, 'and, in any case, when one really covets an object, the price, so long as one can afford it, is immaterial.'

'Is that really your philosophy?'

'Certainly. Besides, the good pastor got rid of the things he really wanted to part with, the things, in fact, that he was almost over-anxious to get rid of.'

'What, those ungainly fire-irons?'

'Yes. If I mistake not, he believes that *this* steel poker, and not the brass one which was found at the bungalow, was used to disfigure Miss Minnie's face and head. He had to identify the body, you know, and the fire-irons seem to have come from Weston Pipers, so I think he may have put two and two together and come to a very unwelcome conclusion and possibly a correct one.'

'What was that rather grim picture you tried to buy?'

'A kind of totem, I think, of an obscure and possibly obscene religious sect. I did not want the picture. I only wanted to find out whether he was prepared to sell it.'

'And he wasn't. What did it represent?'

'The phases of the moon. Had it been sculptured instead of painted, there might have been a fourth face at the back of those three which were depicted.'

'Black magic?'

'A magical conception, anyway. The picture represented the Great Mother of the ancients. She belongs to a form of witchcraft innocent enough in itself in pre-Christian times, since it was a form of worship. Fertility, the bounties of nature and, indeed, life itself were worshipped. It became debased later, partly owing to persecution and the need to go underground, and partly because, until modern space travel proved that this was not so, there was believed to be a dark side to the moon.'

'So these Pan-whatever lot that this chap leads are really modern witches and Miss Minnie was one of them. I suppose her death wasn't a ritual murder of some sort?'

'I think there was a more rational reason for her death.'

'Too bad! I was hoping for sinister revelations. What's the next move?'

'I shall show the fire-irons to the police. If they accept my theory that among these is the object with which Miss Minnie was struck after she died, no doubt they will visit the shop and obtain from the proprietor a description of the person who sold the fire-irons to him and the date on which he purchased them. If the police dismiss my theory (as they may and it will not surprise me if they do) we ourselves will pay the shop another visit.'

'Won't the chap smell a rat when we go back there again?'

'After we have been customers and I go solely in order to make him another bid for his picture?'

'But you said it was a witchcraft thing and that it must have some significance for this sect he leads.'

'Nothing was said by me or admitted by him along any lines which could connect the symbol with witchcraft. Besides, witchcraft is quite respectable these days. It is even discussed on television.'

'You rather aroused his suspicions. You rather gave yourself away over the yataghan, I thought.'

'In what way?'

'Specialised knowledge and all that.'

'Specialised knowledge of the weapons of cut and thrust does not also imply specialised knowledge of ancient pagan cults. In fact, the one may allay suspicion in the case of the other. Now, had the yataghan been an *athame*, there might be some substance in your argument.'

'Let it go! Let it go! You know, I'm beginning to think I'd like to see the chap's face when we turn up again and are in the market for that picture.'

'It will be inscrutable, I fancy. Now I come to think of it, we could go back there after lunch. There is no reason for me to be in a hurry to show the police my fire-irons. There will be no fingerprints on them now except those of the shopkeeper and myself.'

'Oh, I don't know so much,' said Laura doubtfully, 'about losing time. After all, I *am* a Scotland Yard wife. If I stalled on showing the police anything which might help an en-quiry, however indirectly, Gavin would be livid, and quite right, too.'

'Very well, I will give up my treasure-trove tomorrow, but if the shopkeeper has any guilty knowledge he will swear that Niobe Nutley sold the fire-irons long before Chelion Piper returned from Paris.'

The police showed what Laura, who had expected rather more to come of Dame Beatrice's exhibits, thought was a luke-warm interest in the fire-irons, for, as the Chief Superintendent pointed out, nothing was to be gained from them in the way of fingerprints.

'We didn't think the poker found in the sitting-room at The Lodge was the weapon used to batter the head of the deceased,' he said, 'since the prints on it were those of Mr Evans, who admitted handling it, superimposed on those of the dead woman herself. Our theory is that, like so many lonely old ladies, she kept the poker by her as a means of self-defence, picked it up when she heard her murderer enter the bungalow and was disarmed by him before she could use it. In fact, she may have laid it down again when she saw that the visitor was Piper, from whom she anticipated no harm.'

'You still think Mr Piper guilty?'

'Somebody got in who had a pass-key, Dame Beatrice. Except for the window which Piper smashed when he and the other two broke in and found the body, there were no signs of any other forced entry.'

'If Mr Piper had a pass-key, why, in your opinion, did he not use it instead of breaking a window?'

'Oh, madam, you know the answer to that, just as well as we do. To our minds, it clinches matters.. He was hiding the fact from his companions that he had a pass-key and could get into the bungalow whenever he liked.'

'Did you ask whether anybody else in the house had a pass-key?'

'We did, and Miss Niobe Nutley immediately produced hers. Of course, we didn't find Piper's key. Miss Nutley said he had had one and must have lost it.'

'That young lady thinks of everything,' said Dame Beatrice. 'Did you find Miss Minnie's own door-key?'

'Yes, it was on the body. Why do you ask?'

'Oh, nothing – except that Mr Piper clearly was not the only person who could obtain access to the bungalow whenever he wished to enter it. There is another point, too, which you might care to consider: Miss Nutley also used her key (a master-key to which, as housekeeper, I suppose she was entitled), to enter any of the apartments at any time. That must have included the bungalow, one would think.'

'Are you offering that as a serious suggestion, Dame Beatrice?'

'Well, it is one which ought to be taken into account, as the charge against Mr Piper is a serious one.'

'This was not a woman's crime, madam.'

'I wonder on what you base that assumption?' Dame Beatrice outlined her theory about the buckets of sea water. 'Miss Nutley may be tearful and may appear distraught,' she concluded, 'but she has the shoulders and the muscular strength of a coal-heaver.'

'But the motive, Dame Beatrice! It is clear, from our enquiries, that Miss Minnie had good grounds for attempting to upset Mrs Dupont-Jacobson's will. Money, more often than not, is the motive behind murder, especially the murder of an elderly person. The motive in this case sticks out a mile. With Miss Minnie out of the way, Piper's inheritance was safe.'

'And with Mr Piper behind bars and serving a life sentence, Miss Nutley's thirst for revenge would be partly if not wholly slaked, I think. Did you peruse the document written at my instigation by Mr Piper?'

'Yes, with great interest, but it did not convince me of his innocence. These novelists have a trick of putting themselves across when they're given a ball point and sufficient paper,' said the Chief Superintendent, smiling at his own omniscience.

'So no sense to be drummed into *that* blighter's thick head,' said Laura disgustedly when they had left the Chief Superintendent's office. 'You'd think that even *he* would have smelt a rat when the police knew that the Nutley woman could get into the rooms (*and* into the bungalow) whenever she chose.'

'I believe we have left him with something to think about,' said Dame Beatrice. 'He is *not* a stupid man.'

'He's got a bee in his bonnet about motive, that's the trouble.'

'And, as he says, he cannot see this as a woman's crime.'

'I suppose Nutley wept all over Chelion Piper when he was arrested.'

'The Walrus wept for the oysters, but it did not prevent him from swallowing them,' said Dame Beatrice. 'My opinion of Miss Nutley is not a high one, but I see her less as a murderer than as an avenging Fury.'

(2)

It was a fairly long drive back to the Stone House on the edge of the New Forest, but, as Dame Beatrice pathetically observed (following the observation with a sardonic cackle of laughter), 'Now that I have been turned away from the stately mansion of Weston Pipers, I have nowhere to lay my head except in my own home.'

'We could have stayed at a hotel in Moretonhampstead or Exeter,' Laura pointed out.

'There is a good reason for going back to Wandles Parva. My telephone number was on the cards I left with Miss Kennett and the proprietor of the antique shop. I shall be surprised if we do not hear something from the latter before we visit him again. I have very little doubt that he knows we went to the police with his Weston Pipers' fire-irons.'

But the call came from Billie.

'If you want to question Elysée, she is with me again. Cassie McHaig trailed them to the hotel where they were staying and staged a *ménage à trois*. Elysée wasn't having any of that, so she's come back. Don't know really whether I'm glad or sorry. Anyway, she's here if you want her.'

'So we can kill two birds with one stone,' said Laura, who had taken the call. 'Billie Kennett's place isn't all that far from the shop.'

'Quite. The shop first, I think, and then to find out what Miss Barnes has to tell us.'

But when they reached the grimy little junk shop it was closed.

CHAPTER 11

The Elysian Fields

'What's today?' asked Laura, looking at her watch. They had lunched in Moretonhampstead and the time was just after half-past three. 'Saturday, isn't it? So it can't be early closing.'

'Some shops do close on Saturday afternoons,' Dame Beatrice pointed out. 'We shall have to wait until Monday. Perhaps the sect of which our friend is the leader keeps the Biblical Sabbath.'

'Oh, well, we can go and see those two girls, so our trip won't be entirely wasted.'

'I am anxious to talk to that antique dealer as soon as possible. We will do as you suggest. After that, well, at this time of year the hotels in such a little town as this are unlikely to be full.'

'Stay a night here, you mean?'

'Two nights, unless the man opens his shop on Sundays.'

'Oh, yes, of course. Oh, well, we always keep overnight bags in the boot, so we can manage all right.'

'Thanks to a splendidly practical arrangement which you suggested a long time ago, yes, we can. So now, with easy minds, to our interview.'

Billie opened the door to them again and said, in a low tone, after she had greeted them: 'Ellie is a bit shattered, so don't expect too much from her, poor kid.'

Elysée was standing at the window with her back to the room when they went in. When she turned round, Laura was not struck so much by the fact that 'shattered' seemed the appropriate word, as that she was so young and so tall. She came forward and greeted them with controlled composure and added, 'Billie has told me why you've come, but I don't think I can help you.'

'Well, we can all sit down and have a drink, anyway,' said Billie. 'Will you have this chair, Dame Beatrice?'

'Well,' said Dame Beatrice, seating herself as she was directed, 'and how did you leave Miss McHaig?'

The effect of this question startled everybody but the questioner. Elysée, who was still standing, gave a kind of croak, put a hand out as though she was a blind person groping for something in a strange environment, swayed and, but for Laura's quick reaction in leaping up and catching her, would have fallen to the carpet.

'She's fainted,' said Billie unnecessarily. She went to Laura's assistance.

'Shove her head down,' said Laura, 'and let's get her into a chair.'

'Right,' said Dame Beatrice, who had regarded the proceedings benevolently. 'And now, my poor child, we will have your answer to my question. Shall I repeat it?'

'No,' said Elysée, as Billie allowed her to raise her head from between her knees, 'I know what you said. When I left Cassie she was lying on the bedroom floor bleeding from the head. The hotel people were ringing for a doctor. Polly told them she had tripped over a rug and hit her head, but she hadn't, of course. He had knocked her down because she'd said things. If she dies, he'll be a murderer.'

'Have you rung the hotel to find out how she is?' asked Dame Beatrice sternly, before hysterical tears could choke her victim's utterance.

'Of course not. Polly told me to stay out of it, and I'm going to.' Elysée put on an air of defiance.

'How can you stay out of it if you were there with him?' demanded Billie.

'I wasn't *with* him. We booked in separately.'

'So you had that much sense!'

'It was Polly's idea. He said he and Cassie had stayed there before, and it was the first place she'd come to, and that's what he wanted, a showdown, and then he'd have done with her for always.'

'Poor old Cassie!' said Billie, in such dispassionate tones that Elysée gave her a terrified glance and this time did burst into tears.

'Well,' said Dame Beatrice, getting up, 'since you can tell us nothing helpful about the death of Miss Minnie, we had better take our leave.'

'Oh, don't go! Don't leave me while she's in this state!' said Billie. 'I could cope when I thought she was only suffering from –' she grinned, but it turned into a clownish grimace – 'the unwelcome attentions of a heel, but if anything's happened to Cassie McHaig, it's a different kettle of fish altogether, because—'

'Nothing's happened to her,' sobbed Elysée, reversing a previous opinion. 'Of course it hasn't! It can't have!'

'If I were you,' said Billie, 'I'd ring up this prizefighting Casanova of yours and get him to give you the latest bulletin. You need only ask to speak to him. The hotel receptionist won't know who you are.'

'She will when she asks who's calling,' said Elysée, sniffing and then blowing her nose.

'Oh, don't be a fool! Give a false name, of course. Give mine. That will tip off this blasted Hempseed – good God! What a name! – that it's you, and he'll be ready with his story by the time they've paged him and he's got to the phone.'

'*You* ring him,' said Elysée. She turned to Dame Beatrice when Billie had gone out into the hall. 'What did you think I could tell you about Miss Minnie?' she asked. 'And why me?'

'Well,' Dame Beatrice replied, 'I will begin by answering your second question. Enquiries at Weston Pipers have established that, whereas Miss Kennett was accustomed to report daily at her newspaper office, you yourself spent at least three days a week in your flat.'

'Well, Niobe Nutley spent seven days a week there and, when she was there, so did Sumatra – not that *she'd* notice anything which went on. Irelath was her whole life, I believe. She didn't really have eyes or ears for anybody else.'

'Quite. As for Miss Nutley, I have already talked to her. Now, Miss Barnes, you are young, emotional and, I would think, kind-hearted. What was your opinion of Miss Minnie?'

'I don't think I formed one. If I thought about her at all, I suppose I looked on her as a poor lonely old thing who didn't get much fun out of life.'

'When you were alone on those three days a week, did you often go out in your car?'

'No, because the days when I didn't have to go up to Town, Billie had the car. Other days she used her moped, but that's not an all-weather vehicle exactly, and anyway, I always think four wheels are much safer than two.'

'So, although you thought of Miss Minnie as a poor lonely old thing who did not get much fun out of life, you never took her for a drive?'

'No. Oh, well, no, not for a drive, but sometimes, when I was driving to the station – I used to go up to Town by train because of parking problems and because Billie used to fuss because she said it was too far to go to London and back in a day—'

'And on the way to the station you happened to pass Miss Minnie—'

'She was supposed to be going out to do her shopping, so, yes, I used to pull in and pick her up. She had to go to the bus stop otherwise and that's a good mile and a half from Weston Pipers – and the buses are very irregular.'

'She appears to have avoided contact with all the other inhabitants of Weston Pipers. Why do you think she made an exception of you?'

'I suppose it was easier to go into the town by car than wait for the bus, that's all. I suppose she had to come back by bus, but there was nothing I could do about that.'

Dame Beatrice said, 'Could not Mrs Evans have picked her up? Anyway, the journey to the station from which you caught your train is about ten miles from Weston Pipers, I believe, so if we subtract the distance she walked before you picked her up, Miss Minnie would have been in the car with you for about twenty minutes, I suppose.'

'A bit more. The roads round here twist and turn and are pretty narrow, and you can't drive fast on them. Besides I promised Billie I wouldn't, not even if it meant missing my train.'

'She seems to take every care of you.'

'She's worse than a fussy maiden aunt! Of course, she's older than I am.'

'That would explain it. She may be a frustrated mother. Some, of course, keep dogs or cats—'

'And in this case, you mean, she keeps *me!* Only she doesn't, you know. I can pay my way very nicely, thank you. Hers, too, if I wanted to, or she'd let me. She's rather a long time on that telephone.'

'I fancy that she is keeping out of our way while I question you. Did you drop Miss Minnie at the railway station each time?'

'No, I never took her as far as that, because the shops were on the way to it, so she got off before we reached the station.'

'Did she chat to you on the short journey?'

'Not to say chat. She asked me whether I ever took hot sea water baths, I remember.'

'And do you?'

'Heavens, no! The hot water from the bathroom tap is quite good enough for me. The papers said she was drowned in sea water, though. Did Piper do it?'

'What is your opinion?'

'Niobe Nutley might have done it. *He* wouldn't.'

'You think that, do you?'

'She's potty on him and if she thought poor old Minnie was going to have the law on him and try to get Weston Pipers and the money for herself, Niobe would remove her from the scene of operations without a qualm, and it's my firm belief that's what she did, not realising it would land Piper in the soup.'

'Interesting. Did Miss Minnie ever confide such an intention to you – that she meant to contest the will?'

'No, and, if she had, the last person *I* would have retailed it to would have been Niobe. She got rid of Billie and me, you know – anonymous letters.'

'That, according to my information, was Mrs Constance Kent.'

'Oh, I know all about Connie Kent. The letters from Niobe were ever so much worse. Billie doesn't know about them because they used to come while I was in the flat and Billie was working. I've never told her about them. I insisted, though, that we had better get out.'

'How do you know that Miss Nutley wrote them?'

'I thought it was obvious. Her reason was the same as Connie Kent's. Both of them were horribly envious just because Billie and I were happy together and they were not happy at all. Connie makes Evesham Evans's life a misery, and her own, too, and Niobe can't get Piper, although she chases him all the time.'

'But you and Miss Kennett were not entirely happy together, I think – not lately, at any rate.'

'You mean because I went off with Polly? Well, Billie is so bossy, you know, and when she told me I was burning my fingers with Polly, I thought, Right. I'll burn my whole hand.'

'Very childish.'

'Besides, I wanted a man.'

'Ah, yes, very natural, of course.'

'I expect Billie was jealous. She got to know, of course. I can't stand jealous people. Can you?'

'I am extremely sorry for them.'

'Well, they're hell to live with, anyway.'

'No doubt. Do you happen to know which shops Miss Minnie patronised?'

'Oh, the butcher, the baker, the candlestick maker, like everybody else, I suppose. Oh, there was one shop she went to which was a bit different. I only knew about it by accident. She'd left her shopping-bag in the car and my train that morning was cancelled for some reason or other and there was an hour to wait for the next one, so I thought I might as well chase after her because she'd probably need the shopping-bag. I parked the car in the usual place outside the station and walked back to where I'd set her down. She didn't walk very fast, so she hadn't got far along the sea-front where some of the shops are, and I could see her in the distance. I hurried up, and saw her turn into a little side street, so I followed and spotted her going into a little, very scruffy antique shop. I went in after her, but when I got inside there was nobody there. I waited a bit, then I rapped on the counter, but nobody came. I rapped again, then I banged and shouted, but still nothing happened. I didn't like just to leave the bag there – it was rather a decent one – so I went back to the car with it and locked it in the boot.'

'So when did you return it?'

'I forgot it until Billie and I had to put our suitcases in the boot when we left Weston Pipers.'

'I see. Well now, Miss Barnes, there are one or two points which interest me very much. Of course you are not obliged to

answer any of my questions, some of which will not please and
may possibly alarm you.'

'Oh, dear!' said Elysée, turning pale and appearing alarmed
even before the questioning began.

'Yes. Remember, however, that I am the soul of discretion
and that my profession has schooled me to keep secrets a good
deal more disgraceful, I am certain, than any of yours can be.
In addition, I assure you that I am unshockable, so fear nothing. You gave Miss Minnie fairly frequent lifts in your car?'

'Yes, I picked her up fairly often,' agreed Elysée.

'Why did you not pick her up outside her bungalow?'

'I suggested it, but she didn't want it that way. She said she
had refused lifts from one or two people and did not want to
offend them by taking lifts from me. Actually, as I now know,
she didn't want anybody at Weston Pipers to see us together.'

'Do you know why?'

'Yes, I do now. That's why I wanted Polly Hempseed to
seduce me.'

'I take it you are unwilling to enlarge on that point, so I will
not pursue the subject for the present. Did you ever go to the
little antique shop on any other occasion besides the one when
you tried to return Miss Minnie's bag?'

'What if I did?'

'I see. You did.'

'I was curious to know why she had gone there and
disappeared.'

'Of course. Did you ever enter her bungalow?'

'Oh, no. I wouldn't have dreamt of trying to do that. She
wouldn't have let me in.'

'You mentioned Miss Kennett's jealousy. Originally it was
not Mr Hempseed of whom she was jealous, was it?'

'I don't know what you mean.'

'I mean that the jealousy was first sparked off when Mr
Piper began to show interest in you. This was some time ago, I
believe, and it died what may be called a natural death when
Mr Piper was arrested.'

'Billie never believed that Chelion killed Miss Minnie.'

'Nevertheless, she was not averse, I take it, to seeing the back
of him. Your interest in Mr Hempseed must have shocked her
very much.'

'I wouldn't know about that.'

'Oh, come, now! Incidentally, the most wounding letter you received came not from Constance Kent, but from Niobe Nutley.'

'I told you that.'

'Tell me, did Miss Minnie never enquire about her lost bag?'

'Actually, when she left it in the car, that was the last time I ever gave her a lift. Anyway, she never asked about the bag and the next I heard of her she was dead.'

Dame Beatrice caught Laura's eye and nodded. Laura put away the notebook in which she had been recording the interview and went to the door. Billie came in and went straight up to Elysée.

'You didn't tell me you'd married him,' she said.

'I had to,' said Elysée, going to Laura for protection, 'but not for the usual reason.'

'Sit down, Miss Kennett,' said Dame Beatrice. 'I gather that Miss McHaig is, at any rate, not dead.'

'Neither is she *Miss* McHaig,' said Billie, her face crumpling up. 'She's married to Hempseed.' She looked at the cowering spectacle of her friend. 'You *utter* fool!'

'I wouldn't have called Billie Kennett a motherly type,' said Laura, when they were in the car. 'Do you really think that she is?'

'I think that, in partnerships such as theirs, one finds a dominant and a submissive; a protector and a protected.'

'In this case, the submissive seems to have cut a pretty wide swathe. Act of rebellion or act of despair?'

'It hardly matters now. Our interests lie elsewhere. I am extremely grateful to Miss Barnes.'

'For returning to that two down, two up, nest of theirs?'

'No. For telling Miss Kennett, in front of witnesses, that she had to get married.'

'And trick that obnoxious Hempseed into bigamy?'

'Bigamy, in my opinion, does not enter into the matter. Mr Hempseed (to use his pseudonym) has far too much common sense for that, I am perfectly sure. I have no doubt that, to satisfy Miss Barnes, some kind of ritual was carried out which she assumed to be a marriage ceremony. She appears to be a singularly guileless young person, and a very bad liar. As I say, I am convinced that Mr Hempseed is far too wary a practitioner to have contracted a bigamous marriage which Miss McHaig could have exposed for what it was at any moment she chose. Also, Miss Barnes saw far more of Miss Minnie than she admits.'

'So what's this "had to get married" argument all about?'

'The loss of her virginity, no doubt, had some importance for her. One assumes she desired to lose it.'

'Oh, well, it isn't fashionable to be a virgin nowadays. How are we going to spend Sunday?'

'In meditation and prayer, as is seemly and right.'

'You're not going to church?'

'Why not? In the business we are about to undertake, the more of the odour of sanctity we have about us, the more sure are we of successfully resisting the powers of evil. Besides, I always go to church when we are at home.'

'Yes, but I thought you looked on that as a social gesture, something the village kind of expected of you as the owner of the biggest house in the place.'

'There is that aspect, of course.'

'Look, what *is* all this? And what has Barnes's virginity got to do with it?'

'That remains to be seen. We shall know more, I hope, when we have visited that sleazy little antique shop again.'

'I say!' said Laura, on a note of enlightenment. 'Does it all add up? I mean, Miss Minnie being connected with that peculiar sect and being seen by that dim-wit Barnes to go into the junk shop and disappear, and Barnes teaming up with this Hempseed simply for the purpose you mentioned, and Miss Minnie getting drowned and disfigured? *Could* it make some sort of sense? I suppose it could. But where does Niobe Nutley fit in? *Didn't* she murder the old lady, after all?'

'Monday's child is fair of face,' said Dame Beatrice, 'so let us see what its pulchritude can do for us the morn's morn, as I believe your countrymen express it. Meanwhile, we are in a seaside town at an unattractive time of year. How shall we disport ourselves on a somewhat cheerless Saturday evening?'

'Go to the pictures,' said Laura.

The cinema, the only one in the little town, looked drab and unprepossessing from the outside, but, in deference, no doubt, to the summer visitors from whom it derived a good deal of its revenue, the interior was warm and tastefully decorated.

The young woman at the receipt of custom looked them over with a casual glance which hardly travelled beyond the treasury note which Laura was holding out, and said briefly, 'One senior cit., one full price – where d'ya wanna be?'

Laura opted for the front of the circle and was picking up her change when, from a curtain which screened the back of the box-office, a bland, expressionless face peered out and a finger poked the girl in the back.

'OK,' said the box-office. girl, without turning round. 'You've got time for a quick one, if you hurry, Dadda. Dirty old man!' she observed in an indulgent tone, when the face had disappeared behind the curtain.

'Who is he?' Laura enquired.

'Name of Bosey. Deputises for me every other Sat' night and Wednesdays, when I go off.'

'I think I've seen his shop.'

'Oh, yes?'

At this moment a considerable section of the audience came streaming out and several patrons came in from outside. Dame Beatrice and Laura mounted one long flight of steps and were conducted down another to their seats at the front of the circle. The main feature was entitled: *The Ghouls of Dead Man's Creek*.

'Very suitable,' said Dame Beatrice. 'At the interval I shall require a choc-ice and a bottle of some obnoxious liquid which I shall imbibe through a straw.'

'When in Rome, and all that, I suppose,' said Laura. 'Sure you wouldn't like me to dash out for some fish and chips?'

There was a message for Dame Beatrice when they got back to their hotel.

'Would you please ring your son at his home address, Dame Beatrice?'

Dame Beatrice did so and was told by Ferdinand Lestrange that, at his last remand before the magistrates, Chelion Piper had been released and the police had withdrawn the charges.

'I don't know whether you or Cox, Cox, Rufford and Cox have pulled it off,' said Ferdinand, 'Congratulations, anyway.'

CHAPTER 12

Discoveries

(1)

Monday morning proved to be as frustrating as Saturday had been. The junk shop was still closed. In spite of the card which hung inside the glass-topped door and announced this, Laura hammered on the wooden panels and then tapped with the edge of a coin on the glass, while Dame Beatrice waited in the car.

Laura returned to it to announce that that appeared to be that and to add that the proprietor either had overslept or else took Mondays off as well as Saturdays and, if the girl in the cash desk at the cinema had spoken the truth, some part of Wednesdays also.

'Anyway, we know he's about here somewhere,' Laura went on, 'because I saw him in the cinema when he popped his head out behind the receptionist. He can't be far away.'

'Monday may be his day for prospecting for more items to display in his shop,' said Dame Beatrice. 'It is not considered by most shopkeepers to be a very good day for trade, I believe. Let us disport ourselves until after lunch as best we may, and return here this afternoon.'

But the afternoon proved equally frustrating. They tried the shop again at two-thirty, at four o'clock and at ten minutes to five, but the notice inside the door was unchanged and Laura's peering in through the glass produced no information, except that the shop was empty.

'We will try again tomorrow,' said Dame Beatrice. Tuesday, however, proved to be another abortive day, so on Wednesday afternoon Laura went back to the cinema on her own to find that the same girl was behind the grille. She seemed disgruntled. She took Laura's money, pushed over the ticket and the change and then hunched herself on her stool and picked up the magazine she had been reading when Laura had come in. The time was half-past three and Laura and Dame Beatrice had been to the junk shop at ten in the morning and again after lunch. It was still closed.

Laura sat through an hour of the programme and then went down to the vestibule. This time the ticket-office stool was occupied by a large man in evening dress.

'Oh,' said Laura, hastily improvising, 'I believe, when I took my glove off to pay for my ticket, I might have left it on the ledge. Would your cashier have seen it and put it away somewhere? It's a brown one, like this – ' she produced one of a pair which was in her handbag ' – and I've only just missed it.'

'I haven't seen it, madam,' the man – obviously the manager, from his costume and unctuous deportment – replied after he had leaned over sideways to glance at the floor, 'but the young lady has only gone off to have a cup of tea. She'll be back directly, if you'd care to take a seat.'

Laura took one of the gold-painted, uncomfortable little chairs which formed part of the *decor* of the vestibule and was not kept waiting long. The girl appeared from behind the curtain at the back of the box-office, she and the manager exchanged a word or two – indignant on the one side, mild and soothing on the other – the manager disappeared behind the curtain and the girl slid on to the stool. Laura came forward with her story of the missing glove.

'You wasn't wearing gloves when you took your ticket,' said the girl. 'You must have dropped it some place else. Perhaps it's on the floor upstairs where you was sitting.'

'No, I don't think so,' said Laura. 'I didn't take anything out of my handbag up there. I asked the man who was taking your place here—'

'The man who was taking my place here, yes, I don't think! The man what *ought* to of been, only he never!'

'How do you mean?'

'Never turned up, the old bugger! And me with a date! I ask you! Wednesday afternoon and evening is my time off and I'd got today planned special. Sours on you, don't it, when you got something all planned out and it don't come off.'

'Oh, dear! I'm sorry. Rotten for you. Does this chap often let you down?'

'No, and better he hadn't, unless he wants my boyfriend waiting for him one night. He doesn't like being stood up, my boyfriend doesn't.'

'None of them do, but perhaps your relief will still turn up. I hope so, anyway.'

She went back to the hotel and explained the situation to Dame Beatrice, adding that, in her opinion, the junk shop proprietor was either out on the toot of the century or that he had scarpered.

'Ah,' said Dame Beatrice, 'our conversation with Miss Barnes had its own peculiar interest, don't you think? A pity that, from the doorway of the shop, the picture in which I took so much interest is not visible.'

'How do you mean?'

'I mean that unless we find some means of entering the shop, we cannot tell whether the picture is still in place.'

'Does that matter?'

'Probably not.'

'I expect there's a back entrance somewhere. Shall I go along and have a look round? There's probably an alleyway from the street and then another one at right angles to it which runs along the back of the shop.'

'I hardly think further investigation is called for.'

'Well, I don't know so much. It's a bit peculiar, to say the least, that the shop should still be closed.'

'Possibly the proprietor is taking his annual holiday.'

'At this time of year?'

'He would hardly close his shop during the months the summer visitors are flocking into the town.'

'If there was another shop next door, perhaps we could ask about him. It's strange he didn't let the cinema people know he would be absent.'

'What makes you so persistent?' asked Dame Beatrice, gazing at her secretary in some perplexity. Laura shook her head.

'Those fire-irons, perhaps,' she said, 'and the murder and Elysée Barnes and one thing and another.'

'Then, if it will ease your mind, you had better find this back entrance, if it exists, but please stay on the right side of the law.'

from which splashes of red ink appeared to denote drops of blood.

'So?' said Dame Beatrice to the doll. She left the shop and mounted the main staircase, being careful not to touch the banisters. The landing disclosed an open doorway. She looked in. It seemed that the chamber was a bedroom and nothing more. The bed was made, the furniture was simple and the room was clean and tidy.

Next door to it was a bathroom and then a short flight of stairs led to two more rooms, one over the shop and the other, the nearer, over the office. The door of the nearer room was open, that which was over the shop and looked out on to the street, was closed.

Dame Beatrice looked in at the open doorway and discovered that, by the removal of the party wall, the two rooms had been knocked into one. Thick black velvet curtains hung at the front and back windows, but were drawn back so that there was plenty of light in the rooms, despite a somewhat overcast, wintry sky.

Around the two long walls and on either side of the window a frieze of life-size nude figures had been drawn in black paint. They were alternately male and female, but there was nothing lewd or in any way remarkable about them. In fact, Dame Beatrice thought, they were the work of a quite considerable artist and although the first effect was somewhat startling, it was not repugnant.

The floor of the room presented another and a more sinister appearance. It was covered from wall to wall in black carpeting on which had been drawn a white circle contained within a square. At each corner of the square were cabbalistic designs which could be interpreted by any student of the occult. The circle itself was bare, but between it and the window was a long, heavy table, painted black and having at one end what appeared to be a headrest padded with white velvet and having embroidered on it in red a facsimile of the goat's head which Dame Beatrice had seen downstairs on the piece of paper pinned to the doll.

Also on the table, laid out in what appeared to be ritual fashion, were a long knife, a sword, a large silver cup, a nine-thonged scourge, a glass jar containing a white substance which Dame Beatrice identified as salt (although she did not attempt to taste it), a carafe of colourless liquid which, from her knowledge of witchcraft, she diagnosed as water, and a V-shaped metal object up the arms of which two serpents, joined at the tail, were climbing. There was also a tall, curiously-ornamented metal cabinet, but it was locked.

Experimentally Dame Beatrice walked behind the table and pulled the cord which operated the black velvet window curtains. Immediately the curtains in the other half of the room also came together and the dim red light from a chandelier, which switched itself on as the curtains closed, balefully illuminated the scene.

'Very pretty,' said Dame Beatrice. 'Black, rather than white magic, I fancy, with overtones of Satanism and, for good measure, a splash of voodoo.' She pulled the cord again to draw the curtains apart. The light extinguished itself and, after a last look around, she went downstairs and into the shop.

When the police arrived she put a handkerchief over her hand before she drew the front door bolts and let them in, although there was not likely to be any evidence, she thought, that the murderer had been the last person to handle the bolts.

The police superintendent wasted no time. 'Serious ma'am, so Mrs Gavin said.'

'A dead man. This way,' said Dame Beatrice, going towards a door at the back of the shop.

'When we heard it was the chap who kept the shop here, we smelt a rat.'

Dame Beatrice looked at Laura, who said:

'Sorry, but I had to give this address and the police insisted on a detail or two. I didn't say the chap had been murdered.'

'It has not been established that he died by the hand of another,' said Dame Beatrice, 'not yet.'

'Anyway, I've brought my boys and the police surgeon has been notified and will be here at any minute, so if you two ladies would show us where the body is, we'll get weaving,' said the Superintendent.

Dame Beatrice conducted him, the fingerprint expert, a sergeant and the official photographer to the office. The fingerprint expert got to work on the room, the sergeant, wearing gloves, methodically turned out the desk and the filing-cabinet, the photographer stood by, waiting for orders, the Superintendent and Dame Beatrice studied the blood-soaked figure on the floor.

'All right, Ford,' the Superintendent said. 'Take from all angles. The knife is still in the body, but it looks like murder all right. And I'm not altogether surprised,' he added, leading Dame Beatrice out of the room and away from the sweetish, horrible stench of decay. 'We've thought for a long time that this shop was a cover for something illegal, but we've never been able to pin down what it is. We got a tip-off from the local manor of his last place of residence, which was in a suburb of Manchester. They hadn't been able to get anything on him, but they'd have loved to pull him in.'

'To the local police station, you mean? Well, Superintendent, perhaps what I have to show you upstairs may interest you, although, since the Witchcraft Act was repealed, it will not be so significant as it might have been before 1951, and most certainly before 1736.' She led the way to the staircase, followed by the Superintendent. Laura, who had stood aside at the doorway of the office to let them out, hesitated a moment, but, impelled by curiosity and having received no orders to remain downstairs, followed them up the staircase.

The Superintendent looked around the walls decorated so startlingly with their nudes and then he looked at the carpet with its white painted square, its circle, its pentagrams and other magical devices, before he turned his attention to the witches' altar.

'I suppose that table would be moved into the centre of the circle when anything was going on,' he said. 'Oh, well, that metal job must be hiding something – a special cup, I daresay – but it's locked, so we'll have to wait before we get it open. Anyway, it ought to yield some very nice dabs, although I bet they'll only be Bosey's own. Well, it's a very elaborate ⸮ Dame Beatrice, and hardly tallies with the junk shop downstairs. Neither does the office, for that matter. He can hardly have needed that expensive desk and a big filing-cabinet for the amount of antique-dealing he did. Ah, well, there may be a lot of perverse nastiness attached to this Satan's Circle, but I can't spot anything criminal about it, unless we can get him on a charge of procuring, and that's no use now he's dead.'

'Ah!' said Dame Beatrice. 'Sacrificial virgins! Dear me!'

'Elysée Barnes!' muttered Laura in the background. 'Gosh! That would explain a lot.'

The Superintendent did not seem to have heard the slight mutterings, but when they had returned to the ground floor and the Superintendent, a handkerchief over his hand – 'although I expect Davis has dusted everything off in here already, to get any dabs there may be – not that they'll help us much, I'm afraid – ' had drawn back the bolts to let the ladies out by the shop door, Dame Beatrice said, when they were settled in the car:

'Elysée Barnes? Yes, it all ties up very nicely.'

'Do you really think she was mixed up in this business? She didn't seem at all the type to me. Anybody ass enough to rush into marriage for the reason she more or less gave, is too much of a rabbit to be mixed up with what could be black magic.'

'If there were no rabbits there might be no stoats,' said Dame Beatrice, 'and to that extent the rabbits may be deemed to be culpable. Girls are enticed to embark upon evil courses because human nature, even when revolted by evil, has a devouring curiosity about real wickedness. Before they realise what is happening, these rabbits are petrified and rendered helpless by the stoats and then (to change our metaphor back into human terms) they are first victimised, as I say, then perverted and at last either discarded or, in extreme cases, murdered.'

'But that only refers to young girls, not to young men.'

'In a different way, men are corrupted too. The balance of their minds is upset and they find themselves taking part in doings which are more like a madman's nightmare than any course of conduct they had ever visualised.'

'Seems to me there must be the germs of corruption, anyway, in such men and women. It can't just be nothing but curiosity in the first place.'

'Well, you may be right, but, of all things, I think that witchcraft has its own fascination. The old gods may be dead, but, in the words of Miss Gracie Fields's deservedly popular song, they won't lie down.'

'Of course, witchcraft is no longer against the law, as you said. I believe there are dozens of covens in England alone.'

'And numberless fertility rites outside them, although their practitioners nowadays seldom recognise them for what they are. At risk of causing you a certain amount of disappointment, I will go alone to visit Miss Barnes for this second time.'

'She'll be more likely to talk to you on your own, you think? I guess that's so. Anything useful I can do while you're gone?'

'Yes, if you will be so good. Nothing may come of your errand, so I must warn you against more disappointment. I should like you to take your yataghan to Weston Pipers, tell Niobe Nutley where it was purchased, but do not, of course, mention that I was with you when you bought it, and ask her whether it has a history. She will tell you that she knows nothing about it, since it did not come from Weston Pipers, which, I have no doubt, is true.'

'Then what?'

'In the words of one of the ancient ballads of which you and I are fond, "and do you stand a little away, and listen well what she shall say".'

'*Willie's Lady.* You don't think Niobe is a *witch*, do you?'

'There are less likely possibilities. Of course, do not press your point about the yataghan. I trust to your discretion.'

'Implied rebuke noted and digested.'

'Neither implied nor intended.'

'Right, then. I'll be an auditor.'

'An actor, too, perchance, if you see cause, but *prenez garde,* as Abbie would say. First, however, we have to explain ourselves further to the police – or so I fancy. There was an unfathomable expression upon the Superintendent's bland and otherwise benign countenance. He will want to know more about our researches.'

CHAPTER 13

Another Case for the Police

'So here's a pretty kettle of fish,' said Laura to the Detective Superintendent. 'A nice thing for the wife of an Assistant Commissioner at New Scotland Yard to go about the place snooping in at windows and discovering dead bodies.'

'Mustn't pull your rank, you know, Mrs Gavin,' said the Superintendent, with an avuncular smile.

'I must. Otherwise you might think I'd done the job myself,' retorted Laura. 'I know you lot! The first person on the scene is also the first to be suspected.'

'Oh, no. That honour, ma'am, goes to the *last* person known to have been present. I may tell you – but this is not for publication at present – that our investigations into the death of Miss Minnie have caused us to keep a wary eye on this Black Magic gang, and even now that this Bosey whom we think was their leader has gone, if we can catch them putting even half a foot wrong, it's curtains for their organisation, because we shall jug the lot of them. They wouldn't be any loss to society, I assure you.'

'You haven't really got anything on them yet, then?'

'Only simple faith that they're up to N.B.G. That goes especially for Minnie and this Bosey who kept the junk shop. We've been able to trace their movements over the last ten years or so, and everywhere they went there are histories of missing schoolgirls. Those two beauties are out of it now, but the rest of their crew must have guilty knowledge of what went on. Of course, girls do go missing, the silly little what-I-won't-describe, but the coincidences occurred a bit too often to be ignored, and we were getting ready to crack down on this little organisation when this chap, who seems to have been the boss-cat of a very dirty alley, got himself bumped off.'

'Or bumped himself off,' put in Dame Beatrice, who, by previous agreement, had left the opening exchanges to Laura as the person who had first seen the body.

'As you say, ma'am,' said the Superintendent noncommittally. 'That could be so of course. Only thing is that those milk bottles seem to tell a different story.'

'Have you spoken to the milkman?'

'We have, ma'am. Most of his ilk are sharp-witted fellows who soon smell a rat if milk is left on a doorstep, especially if the householder is elderly and lives alone. This chap seems to have been an exception. He's also an auxiliary. The regular deliveryman happens to have been down with flu during the period under advisement. This chap says he noticed that two bottles hadn't been taken in, and that there was a CLOSED notice on the shop door, but he didn't know what to do. He left the third bottle, but had wit enough to report at the depot. They told him not to leave any more, but, the next time he called, all the bottles had disappeared. However, he obeyed orders and did not leave any more milk, figuring that the customer, with three bottles in hand, was hardly short of milk and would contact him when he wanted more. All the householder had to do was what most of us do, just stick a note in an empty bottle, but Bosey doesn't seem to have done this.'

'Apparently not, Superintendent. I spoke to the man myself on one occasion.'

'The milkman? Really, ma'am? How was that, then.'

'Mrs Gavin and I had visited the shop and she had made a purchase. In the back of the shop I had seen a picture which, I thought, had magical connections and I wanted to persuade the proprietor to sell it to me, but the shop was closed. Although there was no milk on the step, I noticed that the man did not leave any.'

'Well, the bottles do pose a problem, Dame Beatrice. Now, ma'am, the doctors (we had two of them, our own and an outsider) agree that the corpse was at least three days old when they examined it, so who but the murderer took in the milk?'

'These are indeed deep matters, Superintendent.'

'What we and our colleagues in the other parts of the country where Minnie and this man are known to have lived are doing next is to check up on the parents of the missing schoolgirls. One of them – one of the fathers or boyfriends, presumably – may have got to know something of these Satanists' nasty little activities and trailed them down here and exacted a private vengeance, and if what we think happens to be true – molestation of virgin girls after kidnap and followed by the ritual death of the victims – well, speaking ex-officio, I damned well don't blame him. Still, my job is my job, and, if I can find him, it's my job to bring him to book.'

'Were there fingerprints on the milk bottles?'

'Yes, but nobody's that we could check up on. That's the worst of murder. Unless there's direct evidence and provided the man or woman only does it once and has never been in our records for any other crime, fingerprints don't mean a thing.'

'What about the weapon?'

'It was sticking into him. It was a broad-bladed kitchen knife and as sharp as a razor. He was sitting at his desk, we think, and the murderer sneaked in – probably from the shop if it was open – and caught him napping. Then either he fell or was tumbled on to the floor the way you found him. Well, he deserved what he got. He was a swine all right, if we read the papers in his desk and filing-cabinet correctly. They were in code, of course, but our experts soon broke it down and the details, although given in what we believe is a very low key, were horrifying enough, in all conscience. If somebody *did* take the law into his own hands and kill a monster, well, as I said, I'm only too sorry it's my job to catch the fellow, that's all.'

'It is a pity the shop is comparatively isolated,' said Dame Beatrice. 'You might have obtained useful information from the neighbours.'

'He was too fly a bird to want neighbours, ma'am, with the kind of doings we reckon went on in the top-floor rooms of that shop. A well-meaning party in the next street, Number Twelve, contacted us but wasn't helpful.'

'I take it that the question of suicide is not ruled out? People do stab themselves, and a nice mess some of them make of it,' said Dame Beatrice.

'Suicide? But I'm sure we've been very careful not to ring any alarm bells. No, my view is that some father with a real grievance had been brooding over things until he couldn't live with himself until the deed was done. My God! If one of those schoolkids had been *my* daughter, I'd have finished him off myself and be damned to my career and everything else!'

'A man of blood and iron,' said Laura, when they had left the Superintendent.

'A man whose professional training has not warped his social conscience. Well, there are various steps which you and I can take. First I want another talk with that milkman.'

'If he's as moronic as the Superintendent thinks, he won't be much help. In any case, I expect the regular milkman is back on the round by now. Influenza doesn't last all that long unless you die of it.'

'There speaks the heartless healthy.'

'Nonsense! I have every sympathy with illness. Well, if *you're* going to seek out the milkman, what do you want *me* to do?'

'Do nothing at all, and in your own masterly fashion, just for the present. Later on I shall be requiring signal service from you. You will have to conduct an interview which in your hands may bear fruit, but from which I myself should most probably obtain nothing at all.'

'If you still suspect Niobe Nutley of murdering the Minnie woman, who killed the shopkeeper? Niobe would have had no motive for that.'

'Who knows? – although I think you may be right. Besides, I no longer suspect Niobe any more than others I could mention. Since we discovered the antique shop and its varied contents, including the dead body of the proprietor, my range of suspects has been considerably widened.'

'You don't really think the police believe Bosey performed human sacrifices, do you? It seems utterly incredible to me.'

'It is not incredible at all. As we have reason to know, there are monsters among us. I am afraid that the Superintendent's observations on the matter are of the utmost importance and it is more than possible that whoever killed Bosey (unless he committed suicide) may have scotched the snake, not killed it. Oh, I am quite certain that the Superintendent's remarks were far more than lurid hints. I think the police were closing in on these so-called Panconscious People and I think the death of Miss Minnie is proof of that. Well, now, if you will stay in the hotel tomorrow and await my return, I may come back with news. There may be telephone calls while I am out, so it will be as well if somebody is available to answer them.'

George drove her into the town next morning and parked the car outside the house nearest to the shop, the number twelve mentioned by the Superintendent. Dame Beatrice rang the bell and asked whether the milkman had called that morning, adding, with specious truth, that she had not seen him that day. The housewife, a kindly body with a strong local accent, stated that the milkman had left her herself a pint bottle, as usual, and that it was 'the right man on the round again, and not that silly boy who was always making mistakes'.

Had the woman any idea of the time of day?

'When he called? No, not to half an hour or so, I haven't, but he was in the road when I went out shopping at ten, and my milk was on the step when I came back about eleven.'

'Oh, thank you so much. I am sorry to have troubled you. No doubt they will be able to supply me with milk at the supermarket.'

'Anyway, you're welcome to come in and have a cup of tea, my dear. You must be desperate for one.'

Dame Beatrice went in and, over very strong tea and a home-baked scone, she and her hostess were soon deep in conversation. Dame Beatrice admitted to being a newcomer to the neighbourhood and, to avoid any reference to her present address, stated that she had spent a short time at Weston Pipers.

'You probably know it,' she said. 'It is a very large house in the next village and has been converted into flats.'

'I expect you left there on account of the murder.'

'Yes, chiefly that, but I also found it very expensive.'

'Did you know the party who was murdered?'

'I do not think anybody knew her. I am told that she kept very much to herself. In any case she was dead before I arrived.'

'The murderer must have known her, mustn't he?'

'Unless he was a burglar and killed her so that she should not scream and raise the alarm.'

'A burglar? Oh, well, in a rich place like Weston Pipers might well be, but that couldn't be so with *our* murder, could it?'

'*Our* murder?' (The subject had come up easily and early.)
'Oh, you mean the man who kept that little shop on the
corner. No, I shouldn't think there was much worth stealing
there.'

'A load of old rubbish, that's all. But he had other irons in
the fire, so 'tis said.'

'I heard he used to work at the local cinema.'

'Oh, that was only very part-time. No, there used to be cars
parked in this road after the shop was shut – big cars, some of
them – and ladies in evening dress. We reckon he used to run a
gambling place. The police came once or twice, but it seems
they never found anything that shouldn't have been there, and
there was never noise or anything to complain of. Perhaps he
was licensed or something, and the police couldn't touch him.'

'The police have been there again, I suppose, if he was
murdered.'

'Oh, yes.'

They discussed the gory details with relish.

'Somebody who owed him gambling money, I wouldn't
wonder,' said the woman. 'Debts of honour they call them,
and you can't be made to pay, I don't believe, but still no need
to murder him, was there?'

'Did nobody but women in evening dress get out of the cars?
Were there no escorts?'

'Now and again there would be gentlemen. There was one
little tiny fellow I saw a couple of times. I only noticed him
because he was so very small. Like a little doll he was. Of
course it wasn't the same lot come every evening. It was as if
they all had their special times. I suppose there wasn't much
room for them all to come at once.'

'Were any of the women noticeably tall?'

'Tall? Oh, yes, a couple of them were, but the pretty one
only came during the day. She was a good deal younger than
the other. They never came together, not so far as I'm aware,
and I haven't seen the older one for weeks.'

'Did you ever see a *much* older woman go that way in the
mornings?'

'Well, not very recent I haven't. She used to come along
some mornings – not every morning it wasn't – and I reckon
she used to go to the shop to do a bit of cleaning. Hurrying

and scurrying she used to be, and with her head down as though she didn't want to be noticed or to stop and speak to anybody. Her clothes was quite good, but sort of old-fashioned, as though she was poor but respectable and as if she'd known better days. Perhaps she hurried along because she felt that doing a cleaning job kind of demeaned her, though what I always say is that honest work is honest work and don't demean anybody, not if they was the richest in the land.'

'This, you say, was on certain mornings. You never saw her in the evenings, I suppose?'

'Oh, well, yes, but it would have been months ago. That's when I see her with the older one of them two tall ladies. They come together in one of the cars I mentioned, but I only see them once or twice, though there might have been times when I *didn't* see 'em. Them times I did see 'em, the old one was still dressed the same, that's how I recognised her. She was acting more like a chaperone, I suppose, though that do seem a bit out of date these days, don't it? But it was mostly in the mornings I see 'em, and not together then they wasn't, the tall one in the same car, which she left a bit beyond my front windows but still in this street, and the old one on her own, like I said, scurrying along on foot. But I haven't seen anything of her for quite a week or two lately, so I reckon either she give up the cleaning job or else he sacked her.'

'But you can't be sure that either she or the tall younger woman visited the antique-dealer's shop, can you?'

'Well, being as you ask me, dear, yes, as it happens, I *can* be sure. Mind you, most times I only see one or other of 'em by accident, like as I might be cleaning my front windows or doing a bit of dusting in there, but sometimes I would have my hat and coat on to do my shopping early, and I walked up the street instead of down it and had to come past the shop and then there's a flagged alley, a bit further along, which takes you down to the shops along the front.'

'And you actually saw one or other of them go into the shop?'

'I did that and with my own eyes. The time I saw the young tall lady, she was carrying a bundle, so I reckon she had tooken something to try and sell. The old one always carried a bag, but I reckon that was only her working overall.'

'But once she wasn't carrying anything, and another young lady came after her with it, but did not catch up with her.'

'Now how do you know that?' asked the woman, wide-eyed.

'Only because that particular young lady was resident at Weston Pipers, and to that extent I became acquainted with her.' Dame Beatrice did not say that she and Elysée had not been resident at the same time, but the woman asked no awkward questions and they parted with mutual expressions of goodwill.

'Heaven bless the uneventful lives of home-based women,' said Laura, when she had heard the story. 'They notice everything, they remember everything and they often add up correctly. So you didn't see the milkman?'

'There was no point, since he is the wrong milkman. In any case, I do not think the one the police interviewed can be of any further help. All the same, I think this kindly and unsuspecting soul I visited has advanced the enquiry a little. She may have established a definite connection between Niobe Nutley and Miss Minnie. This, I imagine, would have been when Niobe made the excuse of coming to the town to bathe from the beach here. Were there any telephone calls?'

'Yes, there was one from Billie Kennett. She rather wanted to know what we were up to, I think, although she didn't put it as baldly as that. She did say that, although she and the Barnes girl have teamed up again *pro tem* she doesn't think it will last. Reading between the lines as an experienced woman of the world and the mother of a newly-married daughter, it sounded to me as though she believes Chelion Piper has got his eye on our Miss Barnes. At any rate, he seems to have gone to the length of plugging Polly Hempseed in the eye and, knowing what we *do* know, I would call that rather significant, wouldn't you?'

'It is easy enough to read too much into such incidents. I am not an upholder of private vengeance,' said Dame Beatrice, 'but there are occasions on which it has my fullest sympathy.'

'Is this one of them?' Laura enquired.

'No. I am speaking my thoughts aloud.'

'I wonder what the police are doing about those two

murders? From what we know now, they must be connected in some way.'

'Only in one way, of course.'

'Two ways, I would have thought. There is the Satanist angle and also there is the point that both Minnie and this Black Art leader must have been killed by the same person.'

'I admit your first contention. Your second is much less certain.'

'You don't think the same person killed them both?'

'People who kill more than once are apt to repeat their methods. Poisoners continue to poison, stabbers to stab. The two deaths we are considering have nothing in common except death itself.'

'Couldn't it be that the murderer used whatever means happened to be at his or her disposal?'

'Yes, it could be so, of course. Well, I must have a word with the Superintendent. No doubt he will be interested to hear an account of my activities and the conclusions I have drawn from them.'

'May one ask what conclusions you have drawn from them?'

'Well,' said Dame Beatrice, 'one of the conclusions I have drawn is that I think I may be inclined to keep the eleventh Commandment.'

'Which is?'

'Oh, come now! You, who must have been in hot water times out of number at school and you who, as I remember it, were not always a model student at Carteret College of Education, should not need to ask me that!'

'No, honestly, I don't get you. Is there an eleventh Commandment? If so, how come?'

'Certainly there is an eleventh Commandment. Its place of origin, I believe, was Eton College, the pious foundation of King Henry the Sixth.'

'Oh!' said Laura, suddenly enlightened. 'Tell a lie, tell a good 'un, and stick to it. Somehow, though, I shouldn't have thought that kind of thing would be in your line.'

'In the ordinary course of events it would not, but circumstances, to quote a trite saying, do alter cases. With what are we confronted?'

'Two murders.'

'Of two infamous characters of whom the world is well rid.'

'Do you mean you know who the murderer is, and that you're going to cover up for him or her?'

'I mean only that I think I know the identity of both murderers, and I think that one is male, the other female. If I am right – but I still can find objections to my conclusions – for the first I need provide no cover. For the second, well, we shall see what transpires. Edna St Vincent Millay was not resigned to the shutting away of loving hearts in the hard ground. *I* am not resigned to the shutting away of loving hearts in a prison cell.'

'I am fogged and bewildered.'

'I may be wrong in my conclusions, of course, as I say. We must see what impression they make on the police. Of course those milk bottles may prove to present me with a problem. The Superintendent is anything but a fool.'

'But you can't take the law into your own hands!'

'Perhaps I would need to love it before I did that. As it is, perhaps I have decided to ignore it.'

'What have milk bottles to do with your decision?'

'With *my* decision, nothing, but I doubt whether the Superintendent will be content to ignore them.'

'If you're so concerned about the milk bottles, why didn't you shove them into the fridge while you had the chance?'

'They were important evidence on two counts. They gave a pretty clear indication of the day, although not the time of day, on which the antique-dealer died. Apart from that, I had not formulated any theory, when we found the man's body, as to the identity of his killer. I do not know *now*, for certain, who that was, but I have my suspicions.'

'Well, I suppose it's of no use to ask any more questions. Do we go and see the Superintendent again, or shall I ring him up?'

'I will go alone to see him. You, as a policeman's wife, might be wiser to stay out of all future proceedings.'

'If you're going to cook the books, I better had, but you know, Dame B., dear, I'm beginning to wonder whether you and I are on the same wave-length over all this. We *are* talking about Chelion pasting Polly in the eye, I suppose, and the possible implications of that action?'

'*You* may be. I am not.'

'And I'm to stay out of all the fun from now on?'

'That would be expecting too much of you.'

'I'll tell you what I'd love to do, then; I'd like to pay Niobe a visit. I'd like to find out how much she knows about Barnes and Chelion Piper.'

'A delicate subject and one far better left alone at present. Pay her a visit by all means, but take your friend the yataghan with you and be wary.'

CHAPTER 14

The Yataghan

It was an errand altogether to Laura's liking.

'Hope I shan't be arrested for carrying an offensive weapon,' she said blithely. 'I'd better stick it in the boot of the car.'

Dame Beatrice had never described Niobe's physical appearance, so that Laura, who had had nothing to go on except the story of Niobe's almost incessant weeping, was somewhat taken aback when, the all-efficient charwoman having announced her, she was confronted by the chatelaine of Weston Pipers.

Laura, herself an Amazon, taking in Niobe's size, thews and general aspect, thought, 'If it came to a scrap, I don't know that I'd fancy my chances!'

'Mrs Gavin?' said Niobe. 'Do take a seat. I'll look up the books and see what we have. Will you be alone? I don't take children, of course.'

'Mine are grown up and live with me no longer.' Laura, who perceived the misunderstanding, was not going to let pass any chance of seeing something of Weston Pipers while she was there. She added: 'My husband works in London, so is not at home all the time.'

'All the same, no doubt you would want something suitable for two. Excuse me.' Niobe opened a ledger and ran her finger down a closely-written page. 'Ah, yes. If you would care to come this way.'

'Before we begin a tour of inspection, I should like to know something about terms,' said Laura.

'Oh, they vary from flat to flat, but the most expensive flats are already let, I'm afraid. Do put down your parcel. It looks rather heavy. It will be quite safe here in my office.'

Laura laid the yataghan, which was wrapped in brown paper, across the corner of Niobe's desk.

'A present for my son,' she said. 'He is a collector. I picked this thing up in a little junk shop in that town on the other side of the bay.' She waved towards the creek which was visible from the office window. 'Are those the only grounds to the house? The lawn seems small for a house of this size and that bungalow takes up a lot of room.'

'Oh, that lawn is nothing, except for the view of the sea. The park and gardens, with some ornamental water – a lake, no less – are at the front. Whichever flat you choose will give you an excellent look-out.' Niobe closed the office door behind the two of them and led the way up the beautiful staircase.

'Well,' said Laura when she had been shown the rooms previously occupied by Billie and Elysée and recently vacated by Dame Beatrice and had also seen the two flats which so far (although Niobe did not mention this), had never been let, 'I don't think this is exactly what I'm looking for. The place seems (if you'll forgive the expression) rather a *rabbit warren.*'

'What!' said Niobe, and to Laura's concealed delight she burst into tears. 'Oh, Mrs Gavin! What a horrid thing to say!' She ran down the stairs to the hall and banged tempestuously at a door. It opened, and a tall, querulous young man stood there. 'Good Lord, Niobe,' he said, 'what's all the racket?'

'Oh, Chelion! Will you take Mrs Gavin into my office to collect a parcel she has left there? She doesn't want a place here. She calls it – she calls it a rabbit warren.'

'No, it's a nest of vipers,' said the young man, with a sour smile. 'Well, if she doesn't like the house, show her the bungalow, and for goodness sake don't interrupt me again. You know I'm writing my prison story for the Sunday papers. How am I to get on with it if you come crashing in every second moment?'

He slammed the door in Niobe's face. She turned her tear-stained countenance to Laura and asked humbly:

'Would you care to look over the bungalow? You would be quite on your own there.'

'Oh, well, as I've come all this way, I may as well see everything, I suppose,' said Laura off-handedly. 'Did I hear you call that man Chelion? It's an unusual name. I seem to have seen it somewhere, and recently, too.'

'Oh, really? Yes, I suppose it is an unusual name. I believe it comes from the Bible, only he spells it Chelion, not Chilion.'

'Ah, yes. Chilion was one of the sons of Naomi, I believe,' said Laura, who had looked it up as soon as she had heard Piper's name. Niobe said how clever it was to know these things. She had regained her composure very quickly, Laura thought. She now led the way into her office and Laura picked up the parcel containing the yataghan. She had taken the precaution of leaving the car outside the gates of the mansion in case any of the inhabitants of Weston Pipers, particularly Niobe herself, should recognise it as that which had brought Dame Beatrice to the house. For the same reason, she had been her own driver and had left George behind.

'You mentioned a junk shop in the town,' said Niobe, as they walked across to the bungalow.

'Yes, a rather wretched little place up one of those streets which go uphill away from the front. I picked this thing up and they also had a rather nice set of fire-irons which they said came from this house.'

'From Weston Pipers? They couldn't have done! We have no coal fires here.'

'Perhaps, before it was converted into flats—'

'Oh, I see. Yes, perhaps. I suppose you noticed that all the fireplaces had been blocked up.' She produced the right key and opened the bungalow door. 'Well, this is it. Look round all you want. I'll wait in here.'

Nothing loth, for, like many people, she was possessed of a certain amount of curiosity concerning places where murder is known to have been committed, Laura went on a tour of inspection. There was not much to see. The place was sparsely but just sufficiently furnished, the bed (presumably the one in which George had slept) was new, and there was no sign of any of the pails in which Miss Minnie's sea water had been collected and in one of which, according to Dame Beatrice's theory, she had been drowned.

Laura returned to Niobe, who had stayed just inside the front door and shook her head. She spread out two shapely palms in a gesture of apology and said sadly:

'Not quite what I'm looking for, I'm afraid.'

'No, I thought it wouldn't be,' said Niobe calmly. 'Why did you come here?'

'It was suggested to me by a friend, who happened to be with me when I bought this.' She unwrapped the yataghan, drew it from its sheath and flourished the cleaned and polished blade. 'She thought it might have come from here.'

Niobe drew back in the face of the slightly curved, gleaming, menacing weapon.

'Good heavens! Put that thing away!' she said. 'Of course it didn't come from here.'

'But the fire-irons did,' said Laura, lowering but not sheathing her weapon. 'I suppose you sold them to that shop when you had all the electric fires put in and the ordinary grates blocked up.'

'People in flats don't want to be bothered with coal fires. Anyway, what fire-irons are you talking about?' But there was no doubt that Niobe was both astonished and alarmed.

'Oh, a set which the shopkeeper was so anxious to get rid of that he threw them in for nothing when I bought the yataghan.'

'The what?'

'This thing.' Laura made a pass with it, swishing it through the air. 'There was another thing in the shop which was rather interesting, but the man wouldn't part with it. It was a picture. It looked like – you haven't got a bit of paper on you, by any chance?'

'What for?' Niobe kept fascinated eyes on the naked blade as though it was having a hypnotic effect on her.

'I could draw the picture for you,' Laura explained.

'I'm not interested,' said Niobe, taking a step backward.

'You had better be, or else I shall tell you what else we saw in the shop, yes, and in the upstair rooms, too.' Laura lowered the weapon, but spoke in a menacing tone which she herself rather admired.

'You went upstairs? But there is nothing for sale up there!' exclaimed Niobe, now making no secret of the fact that again she was alarmed.

'You think not?'

'I know there isn't. Besides, the proprietor would never have allowed you upstairs.'

'How do you know that? Suppose I mentioned a room, or, rather, two rooms converted into one? Suppose I described black velvet hangings, a table with various rather suggestive implements laid out on it in ritual fashion, a row of life-like paintings of nudes on the walls—'

'All right! All right! That's more than enough,' cried Niobe. 'You had better come up to the house and meet the others.'

'Oh, you mean Shard and those people,' said Laura carelessly. 'As you wish, but they are of little importance so far as I am concerned.'

'You know them? Then why have we never seen you at a coven?'

'There are covens and covens.' Laura was on very unsure ground and she knew it and hastened to get on to less dangerous territory. 'I don't suppose any of your company here have penetrated very far into the Mysteries. I should still like to test you with my picture. Then we may know where we stand.'

'Oh, I'm hopeless at guessing games,' declared Niobe, emitting something which might be classed as a laugh, but still eyeing the yataghan nervously.

'Ah, come on, now!' said Laura, giving the weapon another dangerous-looking flourish.

'Oh, very well,' Niobe agreed. 'Back to my office, then. I never argue with psychopaths. But I do wish you would sheath that thing. It isn't part of your ritual, is it?'

'No, no, merely a very present help in time of trouble.' Laura put it back into its scabbard and followed her companion out of the bungalow and across the lawn. Chelion Piper was in the hall.

'Hullo,' he said. 'Do we get a new tenant?'

'Not for that morgue,' said Laura decisivly. 'At any rate, not so far as I am concerned. Would *you* live in it, Mr Piper?'

Chelion shrugged his wide shoulders. 'Hardly,' he said.

'Of course, I remember now. It was you who discovered the body.'

'I wasn't alone.'

'I believe not.'

'Here is a piece of paper,' said Niobe, producing a writing-tablet of plain paper. 'Mrs Gavin,' she added, 'wishes to draw a picture she has seen in a junk shop.'

'Oh, yes?'

'Why, Mr Piper,' asked Laura, accepting the writing-tablet and fishing out a pencil, 'have you been released before trial?'

'Oh, at my last remand the beaks came to the sensible conclusion that no case against me would hold water.'

'Unlike the corpse,' said Laura, with intentional bluntness. 'Oh, stop it!' she added fiercely, as Niobe burst into sobs. 'I suppose it was the evidence provided by the buckets of sea water which let you out, Mr Piper.'

'You appear to know things which have not, so far as I am aware, appeared in the newspapers, Madam.'

It was Laura's turn to shrug her shoulders, and the gesture roused Niobe to tearful, sudden, unexpected and impassioned speech. Piper stared at her, said 'Oh, for goodness sake!' and went into his own room, slamming the door.

'Irelath Moore and Sumatra are a couple apart from the rest of us,' Niobe was saying, 'and I'm sure Evesham Evans suspected nothing when Constance paid so many visits to her publishers. And that awful little Shard was always going out to tea—'

'Cassie McHaig must have had some difficulty in hoodwinking Hempseed,' said Laura, boldly chancing her arm and seizing upon this surprising opening.

'Oh, I don't know.' Niobe seemed to be regaining her self-control. 'I had my suspicions of her. She could always make excuses to get out of the house if she wanted to, and Polly had what you might call a static job here and always wrote his sob-stuff letters in his own room. He and Cassie used to have lots of rows and refused to see each other or speak or even go to bed together for days on end.'

'What made you get rid of Billie Kennett and Elysée Barnes?' asked Laura. 'They were harmless, I would have thought, from what I know of them. Anyway, they might have been pleased to be included.'

'Not Kennett. Besides, the Master only co-opted those whom he could trust. Our band—' She dropped her voice and glanced at Piper's closed door.

'*Your* band, yes. The other is somewhat different.' (I am talking through the back of my neck, thought Laura. She only hoped she could get away with what was becoming a gigantic bluff.)

'Different?' said Niobe.

'Yes.'

'Can you tell me more?'

'My drawings will tell you everything you want to know.'

But at this point Niobe seemed to lose her nervousness. She looked narrowly at Laura.

'If you are what you say you are—' she began.

'I have said nothing yet.'

'Oh, but of course you have! If you are what you claim to be, why have I never seen you before?'

'Oh, but you have! That is to say, you have seen my familiar. By the way, before I draw my picture, we need a witness.'

'To what?'

'To the drawing itself, for one thing, and to make sure you don't start any funny business, for another, while I am absorbed in my task.'

'Perhaps you would care to name the witness, since you seem to know some of my tenants so well,' said Niobe, tearful again, but with a sarcastic edge to her voice.

'Certainly. Please send for your charwoman.'

So Mrs Smith was summoned and stood by while Laura sketched the picture with which the junk-shop proprietor had refused to part.

'Yes, fair enough,' Niobe admitted, 'but any ordinary shop-customer could have seen that. It is kept hanging on the wall behind the counter.'

'Just so. I wonder,' said Laura, turning to the interested and puzzled charwoman, 'whether you would be good enough to sign my drawing, Mrs Smith?'

'Who? Me? I don't sign nothing without I know what I'm signing. No small print don't fool me,' said the factotum severely. 'They warns you on the telly.'

'So they do.' Laura put the drawing into her handbag and, unsheathing the yataghan, she asked: 'In your peregrinations round and about this house, have you ever seen this sword before?'

'No, that I haven't,' said Mrs Smith, 'and would not wish so to do. I hate anything of that sort. And now, if it's all the same, my time is worth money and I've still got Mr Targe to do.' She

made a dignified exit. Laura put down the yataghan, but kept
it, still unsheathed, under her hand. With the other hand she
pointed to a chair in a corner of the room but on its window
side, so that, from where she was, she could keep an eye on it
and on its occupant.

Niobe took the seat which had been indicated, and, with a
few swift lines, Laura sketched the evil-looking object which
had taken the place of the picture and dropped some red ink
on it from the bottle on the desk. Then she stood up, picked up
the naked yataghan and moved a little way off from the desk,
indicating, with a wave of the hand and a masterful jerk of the
head, that Niobe, who was clearly in a state of ferment, was to
approach.

'How about that?' she asked, pointing to her red-ink-
spattered drawing.

'Her reactions were rather interesting,' said Laura, recounting
the story of her visit. Niobe's reaction, upon being shown the
drawing, had been to exclaim, 'So you know!' To this Laura
had replied: 'Know what? Like the recent witness, I also read
the small print.'

'Know that the Master of Cups, Wands and Swords is
dead.'

'Upon which,' said Laura, 'she flung herself on to the carpet
and, although she didn't actually bite pieces out of it, one got
the impression that it was only the feeling that she wouldn't
like the taste of it which restrained her. She drummed with the
toe-caps of her sensible ward-shoes and sobbed and sobbed
and sobbed. I left her to it, picked up both my drawings so
that I could show them to you to see what you thought of
them, and left as unobtrusively as possible after I'd
wrapped up the yataghan again. I fancy it proved a real
friend in time of need. Is that why you told me to take it with
me?'

'We live in an age of violence. Soon it will be suicidal for
any woman (or man, either, for that matter) to stir abroad
without ominous means of defence.'

'What do you make of the Nutley reactions?'

'Nothing, except that she knew of the antique-dealer's
death, as she seems to have assumed that you did.'

'So she's a double murderer!'

'It has not yet been proved that she is a single one, of course. We have to remember that the death of this Eurasian warlock may have taken place *after* Chelion Piper's release.'

'Was it because you knew you would be recognised by Niobe and that, possibly, she would refuse to see you, that you sent me instead of going there yourself?'

'That did cross my mind, of course. Besides, I cannot draw pictures. These sketches of yours are masterly.'

'Just little things I toss off while I'm thinking about my next Academy picture. Have I really done any good?'

'You have confirmed something which I had already guessed.'

'About a nest of vipers being, in actual fact, a nest of witches?'

'Exactly.'

'What made you think so?'

'I did not think so until I spoke with Miss Barnes.'

'Spoke *with*? Not spoke *to*?'

'Come, come! Do the prepositions of the most beautiful and articulate language on earth mean nothing to you?'

'All right, then, until you spoke *with* Miss Barnes. Incidentally, I was not surprised that she was young and pretty, but I *was* surprised that she was so tall.'

'She is what is called a model, as well as her having a reputation for possessing literary and artistic gifts.'

'Well, she could give *me* an inch or so, and I'm above average height for a woman.'

'I believe many models are nearly or quite six feet tall. They are thought to show off fasionable clothes better than women of lesser height can do.'

'I call it a damn silly idea. What looks amazingly good on a stream-lined beauty queen of twenty-odd is just plumb ridiculous on a five-foot-three dump of wealthy middle-agery.'

'Your strictures are very just, but now back to work.'

'You don't really think Piper is guilty and that the police arrested the right man after all, do you?'

'Time and my familiar spirit will show. Ah, and talking of familiar spirits reminds me of a conversation I had with Mr Shard soon after I arrived at Weston Pipers. It meant something at the time, but coupled with our visit to Miss Kennett and Miss Barnes, it means a good deal more now.'

'Familiar spirits? All that witchcraft business upstairs in the junk shop?'

'All that Satanism upstairs in the junk shop, yes. There was the strange remark made by Miss Barnes, if you remember, as to the advisability of her contracting a matrimonial alliance.'

'But do you think she *was* a virgin when she decided to hitch on to Hempseed?'

'I have no doubt that a jury of witch-matrons had pronounced judgment and found in her favour.'

'A sacrificial victim! No wonder she was scared enough to take Hempseed for better, for worse! So what next?'

'When I have had a further talk with Miss Kennett, I shall seek out Mr Shard and find out exactly how much he knows. His propensity for spying and "listening ahint doors" may stand us in good stead.'

'I suppose,' said Laura, struck by a new idea, 'all these witchcraft developments won't end in washing out Niobe Nutley from the list of Murderers We Have Known?'

'It is a thought which merits consideration, certainly.'

'Does it put Piper back in the picture?'

'He has never been entirely out of it. He had much to lose if Miss Minnie had lived to pursue her claim to Mrs Dupont-Jacobson's property.'

'Still, he couldn't have murdered the shopkeeper. He was still under arrest when that happend.'

'Was he? You made that point earlier, but nobody knows the exact time of that murder, you know. He certainly had not been killed as recently as on the day that you discovered the body.'

'I suppose the medical evidence will show when he died.'

'Within limits, yes. Actually, I do not suspect Mr Piper, but we must do our best to find an alibi for him if the medical evidence does not exonerate him. But first for Miss Kennett – not that I expect to get any more from her than some confidences regarding Miss Barnes and those lifts into the town which were given to Miss Minnie. This may give us a lead, or it may not. My chief hope lies with Mr Shard.'

'Nasty little man!'

'*Little* is the operative word. He regards his lack of inches in the light of a physical disability, I think, and that gives him a claim on our charity. This "house of dust" in which we are all imprisoned is of such paramount importance to most of us that any blemish or inadequacy in it is a matter of grave concern.'

'Seems dotty to me.'

'Ah, but, you see, your magnificent frame is neither blemished nor inadequate, so you are not qualified to judge the probably misguided but very painful reactions of less favoured mortals, dear child.'

CHAPTER 15

The Witches and Mr Shard

(1)

Billie Kennett was alone. So was Dame Beatrice, for she had left Laura behind, divining rightly that Billie (and Elysée, if she happened to be at home) would talk more freely if an observer and shorthand writer were not present. Laura concurred whole-heartedly with this view and was only too thankful to remain at the hotel, feeling (although she did not express the thought) ill-at-ease in the company of two women who were emotionally involved with one another.

To Dame Beatrice, Billie was not only willing but anxious to talk.

'I first noticed a difference in Ellie about four months ago,' she said. 'She seemed just as keen on our friendship, but somehow I felt that something had gone wrong with the relationship. She had strange moods and there were occasions when I suspected she might be taking drugs. Once I asked her outright if this was so. She denied it, of course, but I wasn't really satisfied. Then she began wanting the use of the car more often than she had ever needed it before, but she said she had made a new contact who wanted her to model ski-clothes for him and she was anxious to do it, so I said no more, but let her have the car whenever she asked for it. I never suspected the Minnie angle, or what she was really up to, of course, or I would have stepped in.'

'And what was that?' Dame Beatrice enquired. 'What *was* she up to?'

'You know enough to be able to guess that. She had got herself mixed up with these black magic people and I think she had gone too far to be able to extricate herself safely. I really do draw the line at black magic. It's horrible. Ordinary white witchcraft cults, well, they're all over the place these days.'

'I think they always were, but I suppose they were kept underground until the laws were repealed,' said Dame Beatrice.

'All comes of this breakdown of orthodox religion, I suppose. Anyway, between true witches and the Satanists there's the same distinction as there is between black and white.'

'Between white and black, surely?'

'Same thing.'

'By no means, but let it pass. So when did you suspect that Miss Barnes had involved herself in undesirable activities? You spoke of four months ago. What happened then?'

'I saw the Satan-marks on her body. When people live cheek-by-jowl in a couple of rooms, as we did at Vipers, and both have a living to earn, you share the accommodation as best you can because time is precious, especially in the mornings, when you've got to get off to work, so if Ellie happened to be in the bath and I wanted to brush my teeth, well, of course, I just went into the bathroom and got on with the teeth-cleaning. One morning I happened to notice some angry-looking marks on her body, one on each breast and one near her navel, so I asked her what on earth she'd been doing to herself.'

'The Devil's signs, of course. In the old days the witches were thought to come by the marks through his agency. What did she say?'

'Passed the marks off as mosquito bites. I was sure they were nothing of the sort, but I had no idea at the time that they were initiation marks. I thought perhaps she had a lover and that they were instances –' her face twisted in a grimace of angry disgust – 'of the divine passion. I was jealous and afraid. I'd felt for some time that she was no longer satisfied with our relationship. I loved her and wanted the best for her, so I accepted what I thought was the situation and tried all ways to find out who the man was.

'I knew she flirted a bit with one or two of the men at Vipers, but I soon dismissed them from my calculations because those of them who would have had any attraction for anybody as beautiful as Ellie were well and truly tied up already, so I wasn't really afraid I was going to lose her to any of them there.'

'Mr Piper himself?'

'Oh, I expect he made a pass or two before they jugged him, but there was nothing in it. I think Chelion is a bit of a monk where women are concerned and I expect he was too thankful to have escaped Niobe's clutches to tie himself up seriously with anybody else. Anyway, I tried my hardest to find out what was going on.'

'And then?'

'Nothing else for a long time, except that Ellie wouldn't allow me ever to see her in the bath any more. I accepted that, the same as I had accepted her explanation about the mosquito bites. Everybody has the option of privacy, and once, as I thought, she'd got a lover, well, I decided to bow myself out.'

'You seem to have behaved with great sympathy and self-restraint.'

'I'm fond of the little so-and-so, and if she wants a man, so be it. Well, the next thing, and much the most important, was this pseudo-marriage with that heel Polly Hempseed. After she had come back here and you had gone, I shook the truth out of Ellie – literally, I mean. I threatened to kill her if she didn't come absolutely clean.'

Dame Beatrice sized up the short, square, sturdy figure and the resolute bull-dog face, and could picture the scene, but she said: 'Wrestling-match or whatever it was, I would have thought Miss Barnes, with her height and the degree of physical fitness which, I imagine, goes with her secondary profession as a model, would have had the advantage in a trial of bodily strength.'

'Not when I'm hopping mad, which I was,' said Billie. 'Besides, Ellie has the usual feminine dislike of going to the mat and settling matters by seeing who can bite pieces out of whom. I think, too, that she was scared stiff of the Satan lot. Anyway, she gave in easily and came clean.'

'How clean, I wonder?'

'Oh, I'm sure I heard it all. I said I should go to the police. She broke down completely and begged me not to involve her. That brought me up all standing, but I got the address of that junk shop out of her and I went along to put the fear of God into that bloke.'

'Interesting. Did you threaten *him* with the police?'

'No. He wasn't there, so I pushed a letter through the shop's letter-box. I couldn't keep on going there. After all, I have my job to think about. Besides, I guessed they had lost interest in Ellie once she had become – once she had lost – after she and Hemp-seed – I mean, she was no use as a sacrificial victim any more.'

'Yes, yes, I quite understand. And now?'

'Well, that's about it. Ellie and I still share this house, but, of course, things will never be the same again. I suppose she'll marry some day. I wish she would, and get to hell out of my life.'

'How does the death of Miss Minnie fit into all this?'

'I have no idea, except that, from what I made Ellie tell me, it was Minnie, blast her! – who introduced Ellie to these Satanists.'

(2)

Niobe herself opened the door to Dame Beatrice.

'Oh, no!' said said, stepping back a pace when she recognised the visitor.

'I fear so,' said Dame Beatrice, stepping inside. 'I wonder whether Mr Shard is at home? It is he with whom I would speak.'

'Mandrake? I expect he's busy.'

'Perhaps you will be good enough to ring through on the intercommunication apparatus and let him know that I am here.'

'Will you state your business? He won't be pleased to have his writing interrupted unless you have business of importance to discuss with him.'

'My business concerns the death of the man who kept an antique-dealer's shop in the town and from whom Mrs Gavin bought a yataghan.'

'A what?'

'And to whom you either sold or gave a set of steel fire-irons, although you have denied doing so.'

'You had better come into my office.'

Dame Beatrice followed her and Niobe made contact with Mandrake Shard.

'Will you go up?' she said. 'He is at the end of the landing on the first floor. There is a nameplate on the sitting-room door.'

Shard, who seemed to have been working at an enormous desk which was covered with reference books, papers and a typewriter which had a half-finished sheet of quarto still sticking up in it, greeted her twitteringly.

'Well, well, well! Hullo, hullo!' he said. 'How nice! How very, very nice! Sherry, I think, don't you? Or shall we go out to tea again? No. Sherry, sherry! Oh, but do come in! Come in!'

Dame Beatrice came in and closed the door. The room, she noted, was beautifully and expensively furnished and, except for the littered desk, exquisitely neat and clean. There was only one picture on the walls, but it was a Picasso of the artist's 1941 period. Dame Beatrice wondered whether its fantastic disorientations, exaggerations and unkind if humorous comments upon a woman's features and bodily attitude were a kind of compensation to Shard for his own tiny but well-formed frame and his loss of the girl he had once hoped to marry.

Dame Beatrice took the armchair to which he waved her and he bustled about in the cupboards of a satinwood cabinet and produced glasses and a couple of early nineteenth-century decanters – all of them collectors' pieces – and cried gaily:

'Which shall it be? Which shall it be? And do you take a biscuit with your sherry? Speak now, or for ever after hold your peace!'

'No biscuit. The sherry is at your choice,' she said. She sat and sipped while she studied the room and Shard, she surmised, studied her. He did not drink.

'More?' he enquired. 'Ah, well, later on, perhaps. One is disposed to enquire, if one does not give offence, why you have come to see me.'

'I want to know more about the Satanists.'

'Oh, but my dear Mrs Farintosh!'

'Since last we met, their leader has met his end. By the way, as there should be few secrets between friends, I ought to tell you that Mrs Farintosh, as such, does not exist.'

'You don't need to tell me, dear and excellent lady. I snooped around, you know, and placed you quite easily since

you are well-known (and famous too), but it seemed only
good manners to respect your alias – or should I say your
nom-de-plume?'

'No, I write, when I write, under my own name.'

'Then welcome to my abode, Dame Beatrice. What do you
want to know about the Satanists? I am hardly a mine of
information, I'm afraid. I attended only two of their meetings
and those were not for the initiated. Targe came to the first of
them with me, but I think he found the proceedings childish
and disappointingly dull. After all, to a man who has the
horrid details of Jack the Ripper's activities propped up beside
his breakfast bacon and egg, the sight of a virgin lying on a
strip of black velvet and having gibberish said over her can
hardly rank as a sexual extravaganza or orgy.'

'But you yourself went a second time?'

'By personal invitation of the Grand Master, or whatever he
called himself. The initiates, when they addressed him (which
they did only after prostrating themselves) moaned at him,
"You, You!" So I never learned his name.'

'Did you ever go to his shop in the town?'

'Well, of course, but not to his shop as such. It was where the
meetings were held, you know.'

'Ah, yes, of course it was. I asked a foolish question. I shall
now ask another. Was the girl on the table someone you
knew?'

'Yes.'

'And did you also recognise any of the circle of members?'

'I thought I did, but we were all masked.'

Dame Beatrice waited, but no more information was
forthcoming. Shard held up the decanter but she shook her
head. He poured himself a glass of orange juice and held it up
to the light (not so much, she thought, to admire the beautiful
colour of the golden liquid as to make sure that she would
admire the beautiful opaque spiral on the stem of the glass
and its bowl engraved with flowers).

Dame Beatrice waved a yellow claw. 'The better the colour
the more worthy of the priceless glass?' she asked. 'Or does the
priceless glass make a most innocuous and healthful beverage
taste better?'

'The second, I think. You are hoping that I will disclose the names of those members of Satan's Circle whom I thought I recognised, but that I cannot do. We were all placed under an oath of secrecy and I am sufficiently superstitious to feel that I cannot break it.'

'It matters little. Your evidence would only be confirmation of what I already know. One thing I believe you can tell me without forswearing yourself. Was the girl on the table the same girl each time?'

'No, she was not, neither was there any masking of her features.'

'And you recognised both girls?'

'No, but I did recognise one of them.'

'Was she unusually tall, as women go?'

'So you know who she was! Dear me! But I have said nothing, mind!'

'No, you have kept your oath. Why did you never go to a third meeting?'

'We were given a date, but Miss Minnie's death caused it to be postponed, so I have never been to the place again.'

'Was any mention ever made of a threatening letter written to the instigator of the proceedings?'

'Not in my hearing. The writer would have been Miss Billie Kennett, no doubt.'

'Ah, so one of the virgins was Miss Elysée Barnes. Thank you for confirming that piece of information, which I already possessed.'

'I have told you nothing,' said Shard. 'Please remember that.' He had been sipping appreciatively. He now drained his glass and set it gently down on the Hepplewhite table at his elbow. 'Quite,' said Dame Beatrice thoughtfully. 'I understand that before Miss Minnie was murdered you believe she sometimes entertained a man in her bungalow.'

'As I told you, I am a dedicated spy.'

'Who was it?'

'As I also told you, I don't know.'

'When you attended the gatherings, did anything in the nature of a Satanic romp occur?'

'Oh, no, nothing of an orgiastic nature at all. The Grand Master gave us some promises, but I understand that we had to wait for the full moon before he could carry them out. The two young women were merely on show to whet our appetites.'

'And Miss Minnie was murdered before he could keep his word. She, I imagine, was his procuress of virgins. If one was sacrificed at each full moon, I should think she was kept busy.' said Dame Beatrice, with an eldritch cackle which made Shard glance at her in alarm. 'I appreciate that you are under oath not to reveal names,' she went on. 'I have seen the room in which the Satanist meetings took place. Apart from the girl herself, was anything else on the table? I may add that I have made some small study of witchcraft, both black and white, so nothing you say will surprise me.'

'Well,' said Shard, 'it didn't surprise me either. One has read the recognised authorities, of course – Ahmed's *The Black Art,* Cavendish's *The Black Arts,* Rhodes' *The Satanic Mass,* Peter Haining's *Witchcraft and Black Magic* and so on – so one knew pretty much what to expect. The meetings were held specifically to get converts, so everything was pitched in a low key not to frighten the neophytes away, but with veiled promises of all kinds of excitement to come. Anyway, in answer to your question, to which I see no harm in giving a truthful reply, there was a gold cup surmounted by a strange device also in gold and terminating in a crescent moon. The cup and this object were placed on the girl's lower abdomen and the Grand Master, bare to the waist and wearing goat-skin trousers reminiscent – ' he gave a falsetto giggle – 'of Robinson Crusoe, sat enthroned behind the so-called altar. There were candles on either side of him and he wore a gold headdress embodying horns with the full moon caught between them.'

'So that, and the cup on the girl's body, were what the metal casket contained,' said Dame Beatrice.

'Did you get what you wanted?' asked Laura, when Dame Beatrice returned to the hotel.

'Yes, and a little more than I expected. Both Miss Kennett and Mr Shard were most enlightening.'

'As how?'

'Ah,' said Dame Beatrice, 'that reminds me! There is one more question which I ought to put to Mr Shard.' She rang through to the hotel reception desk and gave the telephone number of Weston Pipers.

'Bradley speaking,' she said. 'Can you connect me with Mr Mandrake Shard, please?'

A man's voice replied: 'Ah, good afternoon, Dame Beatrice! Piper speaking. How are you? Yes, I'll call him to the phone at once.'

'There is something I have just thought of,' she said, as soon as she and Shard were connected.

'Oh, yes, dear lady?' His high little voice sounded apprehensive, she thought.

'It is merely this: at the meetings which you attended, was there an admission fee?'

'I must admit that there was. Visitors were asked to hand over a fiver each time and we were told that, if we became members, a monthly subscription would be called for. I gathered that the society was anything but prosperous.'

'Thank you for telling me so. I am so sorry to have interrupted your work again.'

'Think nothing of it, dear lady.' The little falsetto voice sounded relieved and cheerful this time.

'Oh, and – shall we say to settle a bet? – I suppose it was you who wrote some of those anonymous letters?'

'Not all, dear lady, not all. Those I did write were great fun, though.'

'I believe,' said Dame Beatrice, when she had put down the receiver, 'that our tiny friend's gift of insatiable curiosity is going to prove a most useful feature of our enquiry. He goes from strength to strength.'

'Dirty little snooper,' said Laura.

'Well, after all, what are *we* but dirty little snoopers, if it comes to that?' said Dame Beatrice equably.

'At least we only snoop so that justice may be done.'

'Justice? She has the two faces of Janus, one moral, the other legal. We may need to subvert her course in one or other of these respects.'

'Here, what are you up to?' asked Laura suspiciously.

'Even I myself hardly know. Our first consideration is to establish an alibi for Mr Piper concerning the murder of the antique-dealer.'

'I thought you were doubtful whether he had an alibi.'

'My doubts are now resolved. The police no longer suspect

him of murdering Miss Minnie and they do not suspect him of so much as knowing the dead shopkeeper, but I have a fancy for the truth and should like to know what it is. Now you would wish to know what passed between Mr Shard and myself. I will give you a full account of it and then we shall see whether your ideas march with mine.'

'They usually follow well behind yours, and limpingly at that,' said Laura, grinning. 'In the old Scots word, unknown to me until I read *Huntingtower* (I think it was), they go hirpling. But I'm absolutely agog. Tell me all, omitting no detail, however slight.'

'After I have had a last talk with the Superintendent, you shall know as much as I do.'

CHAPTER 16

Assessments and Conclusions

(1)

'Oh,' said the Superintendent almost airily, 'we soon gave up our suspicions of Piper and the same – although I can't say we'd ever considered her seriously – any suspicions we might have had of Miss Nutley, the only other person, so far as we could discover, who had ever had a key to the bungalow apart from Miss Minnie herself.'

'Ah,' said Dame Beatrice, 'you discovered, as I did, that those particular keys, Piper's and Miss Nutley's, would not open the bungalow door. But I thought Piper had lost his key.'

'Gave us a bit of a facer when we tried Piper's key which we found in Miss Nutley's desk and she swore was his, and then the duplicate Miss Nutley showed us. Miss Minnie, as she called herself, had had the lock altered unknown to Miss Nutley and Piper. Once we realised that there was no way Piper could have got into the bungalow except the way he did get in, unless Miss Minnie herself opened the door to him – and all the available evidence was that, of all unlikely things for her to do, that was the unlikeliest – we virtually wiped Piper off our slate.'

'But did not immediately release him from custody.'

'An old and perhaps somewhat discreditable ploy, ma'am. We thought that while we held on to Piper the real murderer might get careless and do something to betray himself, but he (or she) didn't, so in the end we had to give the beaks the tip, the last time he was remanded, that we felt he had no case to answer.'

'And you still have no idea of the murderer's identity?'

'No. Anyway, we're now only faced with finding one murderer, not two.'

'Oh, really? You have come to the definite conclusion that the shopkeeper's death was suicide?'

about some of the guests' sleeping habits. There's a crazy streak in that lady, ma'am.'

'A tearful one, at any rate.'

'I don't think her conscience would let her rest. There's no doubt in my mind that she did her best to frame Piper for the murder. I'm almost inclined to put her back on my list of suspects, you know. I reckon she's capable of murder. She's big-built and, for a woman, very muscular. It wouldn't have taken her long to overpower Minnie, who was a little thing and old.'

'I know. I also thought of her at first, but the problem there is that she did not have a key to the new lock on the bungalow until you gave her one.'

'Well, I reckon that's right enough. Mr Piper and Mr Evans let us in after they'd busted a window and climbed in and found the body, and we gave Minnie's own key to Miss Nutley after we'd concluded our investigations at the bungalow.'

'Yes. When I took over the bungalow for a few days, I remember that Miss Nutley's own key would not operate the lock and she was obliged to return to the house for the key you had given her.'

'Well, that only means one thing, ma'am. Except for Mr Piper breaking the window, which he admitted doing, and which we thought at first was a suspicious circumstance, as he claimed he had lost his key to the bungalow—'

'Found later by you and Miss Nutley. At the time, she was ignorant of the fact that neither it nor the duplicate in her own possession, would open the bungalow door.'

'So, ma'am, the suspects are narrowed down in number, it seems to me.'

'Quite so. It appears that Miss Minnie herself opened the door to her murderer.'

'That's it. She must have done.'

'On the evidence we have been given, she made it a point never to open the door to anyone.'

'We only know that from Piper, though. She might have made exceptions he didn't know about. From your own researches of which you have been good enough to keep me informed, it seems that several of the tenants of Weston Pipers had visited that hell's kitchen on the top floor of that junk shop. Couldn't Minnie have been persuaded to let one or two of them into the bungalow?'

'It is possible, certainly, although, except for one person, it seems to me unlikely.'

'And that one person could have been Miss Barnes, who used to give her those lifts into the town and was in the running to become a sacrificial virgin. That's who you meant when you spoke of the murderer slipping through our fingers, wasn't it? You mean she'll have cooked up an alibi.'

'I was not thinking of Miss Barnes, Superintendent. If you remember, you were convinced that this was not a woman's crime and I agree with you. However, I shall know more perhaps, when I have paid my next visit to Weston Pipers.'

'Right. You do that, ma'am. We've still got plenty on our plate trying to trace those missing schoolgirls. Either they or their bodies must be somewhere about. We're still going through Bosey's villainous records.'

(2)

'I am afraid that any morbid discoveries the police may make regarding the fate of the missing schoolgirls will represent but a Pyrric victory,' said Dame Beatrice to Laura, 'since it will have cost the taxpayers a great deal of money and bring less than comfort to bereaved parents, for the prime movers in this truly infernal business are both dead. Do you care to accompany me to Weston Pipers? Do as you wish, for neither of us, I am afraid, is exactly *persona grata* where Miss Nutley is concerned.'

'Nothing would keep me away.'

They went to Weston Pipers, Laura driving, on the following morning and pulled up in front of the house. Early daffodils and late crocuses were showing in the beds under the windows of Niobe's office and Chelion Piper's study, the tide at the foot of the lawn was at the full and the groundsman Penworthy was leaning against the handle of a garden roller watching other people at work.

The work in question was the demolition of the bungalow. Already the doors and window-frames were out and stacked on the grass, and workmen were beginning to load them on to a lorry. A pile of broken glass was lying nearby and other workmen were digging a deep hole in the soft earth at the foot of the high bank near the back of the bungalow as a repository for the glass and any other unsaleable rubbish. Standing by and occasionally dabbing at her eyes with a lace-edged handkerchief, was Niobe.

Dame Beatrice got out of the car, closely followed by Laura, and went up to her.

'Good morning, Miss Nutley,' said Dame Beatrice briskly. 'Rather early, I'm afraid, for a social call, but this is nothing of that kind. I want a word with your man Penworthy.'

'Oh?' said Niobe. 'Well, there he is – ' she raised her voice – 'idling his time away as usual. Oh, good morning, Mrs Gavin. Do you know Mrs Farintosh, then?'

'I work for her, only I know her as Dame Beatrice Lestrange Bradley,' said Laura.

'Well, yes, of course, I know that now, but I knew her first as Mrs Farintosh. There's Penworthy. Help yourselves. Is it— may I know what it's about?'

'Oh, yes, certainly,' said Dame Beatrice. 'It is in connection with the death of Miss Minnie.'

'I see. Yes, I suppose the police are still trying to find out about that, now they've seen fit to release Chelion. I can't think Penworthy will be of any help, though.'

'So you are having the bungalow pulled down,' said Dame Beatrice, gazing admiringly at the orderly nature of the wreckage.

'Yes, it seemed the best thing. I am going to have a heated swimming pool in its place.'

'That, perhaps, will be pleasanter for Mr Piper than bathing from the beach, and will save your own journeys into the town when you wish to bathe.'

Niobe looked suspiciously at her, but Dame Beatrice remained bland and seemed innocent of intending any double meaning. Then Niobe said, as unrestrained tears began to pour down her face:

'Chelion won't be using the pool. He isn't here. He's going to be married. He's left me Weston Pipers and some money. I don't suppose I'll ever see him again.'

'Dear me!'

'I expect it's all for the best.' Niobe began some vigorous mopping-up operations. 'He can't feel any kindness towards me now.'

'I am sorry to hear it. Just a word with Penworthy then, if I may.'

Penworthy, who had heard Niobe's strictures, was now engaged with the roller, but thankfully abandoned his task when Dame Beatrice approached.

'Mornin'!' he said. 'You want to know some more about them old buckets of sea water? Drownded in one on 'em, they says. What you think to that, eh?'

'So you know that, do you? You were a great help, you know. Will you help me again?'

Penworthy wiped the palm of his hand down the side of his trousers. Dame Beatrice took the hint and produced a fifty pence coin.

'I likes to be helpful, I do,' said Penworthy, taking the coin and giving it the benison of a slight spit on the reverse side before he tucked it away. 'What would it be this time?'

'Trespassers.'

'Trespassers?'

'Trespassers.'

'Oh, *them!* Only ent ever been one or two. They come paddlin' round at low tide along the foreshore. Ent nothin' to stop 'em, not at low tide.'

'I am surprised that this only happened once or twice, if it is so easy to get to these grounds that way.'

'Course there might have been more. If I'd been in the kitchen up at the house getting my elevenses, any number could of come and I wouldn't see 'em, but you wouldn't get 'em comin' this time of year. Nobody wouldn't come paddlin' round the creek at *this* time o' year. Come to think of it, though, I do recollect of one what come, but I don't reckon he paddled, 'cos he had his shoes and socks on, you see.'

'How observant you are! Did you speak to him?'

'Ar, of course I did. I said as how he was on private property. He said he had heard a friend of his, Mr Shard, had rented a flat here, and he give me ten p. to go and find out if Mr Shard would come out and speak to him.'

'Did you not think that a very strange request? Why could he not have gone up to the house?'

'He had give me ten p., so I went, but when I got back, me having to go by way of the kitchen, not being allowed the front door, and having to find somebody as was willin' to take a message to Miss Nutley's office to ask her to get hold of Mr Shard, and me 'angin' about only to find as Mr Shard had gone out, well, when I goes back to tell the feller, what does I find but he's gorn. Got tired of waitin', I suppose, and me takin' all that trouble.'

'Can you describe the man?'

'Ar, reckon I can, near enough. He was a shortish, roundish kind of feller with one of them faces, all smooth-shaven and a bit yeller, what look as if they're smilin' until you look at their eyes. Some kind of a foreigner, though you couldn't tell that from the way he talked, and his hair was jet black and quite thick and looked kind of greasy.'

'That is a very good description. Had you ever seen him anywhere before?'

'Not so far's I know. I reckon I'd have remembered him if I had.'

'Now how long ago was this? Can you remember?'

'Oh, that's an easy one. He come the day I took the last buckets of sea water up to the bungalow door. The arrangement was that when the old lady wanted her sea water she put out the buckets first thing in the mornin'. She never stuck to no regular days, but it was always three times a week she had the sea water. Well, I used to fill the buckets as soon as the tide come in and took 'em to her front door and give her a knock and a shout, and then, when she felt like it, which was always in my dinner-time, so I never see her do it, she took 'em in.'

Dame Beatrice took Laura, who had been talking to Niobe, in tow, they drove back to the hotel and she telephoned the Superintendent. He came round at once and listened to the story.

'The description fits Bosey well enough,' he said, 'but there is no proof that he was admitted to the bungalow.'

'It seems to me significant that those were the last buckets of sea water which Miss Minnie seems to have required. Besides, I think, now that we know the connection between them, that

Bosey was the only person Miss Minnie would have admitted
to the bungalow.'

'But why should Bosey have murdered his right-hand
helper?'

'Because he no longer trusted her. She must have miscalcu-
lated in some way, and her usefulness had not only gone, but
she may have brought you and your police force very close to
him. We shall never know the details, but I think it highly
significant that, following his visit, Miss Minnie needed no
more sea water baths.'

(3)

'So now we come to *your* affairs, Miss Kennett,' said Dame
Beatrice.

'They don't bear looking at,' said Billie. 'I suppose you've
got it all worked out. Oh, well, I don't care what happens
now.'

'I hear that Mr Piper has left Weston Pipers to Miss Nutley
and has gone away to be married.'

'Yes, to Elysée. They are going to live in Paris.'

'Very wise. That will take Miss Barnes well away from all
her unhappy memories.'

'They weren't *all* unhappy, you know. It was just that it took
me a long time to accept the fact that Elysée was hetero and
not homo. Are you prejudiced against people who don't
conform?'

'Only against such people – if one is justified in calling them
people – as Miss Minnie and Bosey.'

'So somebody killed Bosey and got away with it. At the
resumed inquest – my paper sent me to cover it – the verdict
was suicide. Anyway, suicide or murder, it was much too easy
a death for that monster.'

'Why didn't you put the milk bottles into the refrigerator?'
asked Dame Beatrice. Billie stared at her. Then she laughed.

'So you know,' she said. 'How did you find out?'

'By inference, deduction and the laws of probability.'

'So what are you going to do about it?'

'Nothing, of course,' said Dame Beatrice, blandly surprised by
the question. 'Who am I to upset the findings of a corner's jury?'

'You mean you're going to let me get away with it?'

'Well, you yourself have stated that it was too easy a death for such a monster.'

'After I'd made Elysée tell me some of the truth – I don't suppose for a moment I got it all – I began to wonder about Minnie's death. I knew it couldn't have been Piper. I did wonder about Niobe Nutley, but I don't believe Minnie would have allowed her inside the bungalow.'

'I agree. When did you kill him?'

'First thing on the Monday morning. Sunday's milk was still on the step, but I left it there.'

'Was the shop open so early?'

'Yes. I got there sharp on nine and he was just opening up. He recognised me, not as Elysée's friend, but as the reporter who'd covered the preliminary inquest on Minnie. I'd met him, you see, when it was over, congratulated him on the way he'd given his evidence and asked him whether he could supply me with anything more about her for my paper. This was before I knew that Ellie was mixed up with the two of them, of course, so the interview was quite friendly.'

'So presumably he left you to look around his shop on that Monday morning.'

'I asked whether I might and he agreed and said he had some paper-work to finish, so would I shout if I found anything I wanted to buy. He went off and I turned the card round on the door so that it said CLOSED, picked up the milk bottle from outside the door, bolted the door as quietly as I could and sneaked along by the way I had seen him go. I had a knife – razor-sharp it was, too – because, of course, I was prepared for a fight when I tackled him about Ellie.'

'You thought you could win if it came to physical combat?'

'I had the knife. He was sitting at the big desk, bent over it, but he heard me and swung round. Then he jumped up and I don't know whether he panicked or whether he thought I'd turn and run, but he rushed me, so I stuck out the knife and that was that. Then I got back as far as the door and fainted.'

'You did *not* faint!'

'Actually, no, but one always puts in a bit of local colour. If I'd been writing this up for my paper, I should certainly have said the woman fainted, whether she did or not.'

'I see.'

'Yes. Look here, you must have had something definite to go on in suspecting me. What did I do wrong? – apart from breaking the sixth Commandment, I mean.'

'Psychologically you were my first suspect, unless (as was possible, of course) some person quite unknown to me had done the deed. My other suspect would have been Niobe Nutley, but I soon dismissed her from my calculations because, far from objecting to Bosey's experiments, I think she enjoyed them because she had to find compensation for Piper's defection.'

'She could have ended up on that sacrificial altar, the same as I was afraid, when I got at the truth, Ellie might have done.'

'I think Niobe Nutley felt that, with her weight and strength, she could have held her own against him if matters went beyond the merely obscene and looked like ending fatally for her.'

'Did you ever suspect Ellie?'

'No. She had taken matters into her own hands to protect her life, even though, in so doing, she had had to sacrifice what some might call her virtue. Besides, I cannot see her as a killer.'

'Yes, that's right enough, I suppose. So what do you want me to do? – give myself up?'

'Why? Your story makes sense. You carried the knife in self-defence and Bosey rushed you and spiked himself on it. Maybe you should not have been carrying an offensive weapon, but that is the most, so far as I am concerned, which needs to be said. But the milk bottles still puzzle me. Can you explain?'

'Oh, yes. I remembered that milk bottles left on the doorstep are a suspicious circumstance, so early on the Tuesday morning, knowing I could get in by the back door because I had left that way, I went along and found, to my horror, not one milk bottle, but two. The bottle I'd picked up on Monday morning must have been left on Sunday and he hadn't bothered to take it in. Well, I shoved both bottles into my brief case – luckily it's a roomy one – made sure nobody was about, went in again by way of the alley and the back door, which, of course, I knew I'd left unlocked, dumped the bottles and scarpered.'

'Well, after all, it *was* suicide,' said Laura defensively, when she heard the story. 'If he rushed her and spiked himself on the knife she happened to be holding, he took a calculated risk and bought the result.'

'Quite. She needs not this spirited defence from you. I accept that that is what happened, although I do not believe it.'

'What will she do now? I'm desperately sorry for the poor blighter.'

'She has her health, her work, and, when she comes to think things over, the satisfaction of having rid the world of one of the wickedest individuals who have ever lived. Not that I wish to exaggerate, of course, but the police are still checking the facts with regard to the disappearance of those school-girls.'

'Do you think he had some idea that Minnie was double-crossing him?'

'I think he distrusted her from the moment she took up residence in the bungalow.'

'But why?'

'She was there for one reason only, it seems to me.'

'To push her claim to the Jacobson-Dupont property by looking for a lost will?'

'Exactly. From that time onwards he suspected that she was putting her own interests before his and, with the police hot on his trail, he could not afford to have a traitor or even a dissident in his camp. I think he came more than once by night to the bungalow, no doubt to put his case. Mr Shard, the self-appointed spy, knew of those meetings and, although he refused to name the man to me, claiming that he did not know who it was, I am perfectly certain that he *did* know. He had attended at least two of the Satanist meetings and must have heard Bosey speak at them.'

'But didn't you tell me that Shard accused Piper of the murder?'

'Mr Piper was, unwittingly perhaps, the cause of envy and jealousy. Miss Nutley seems to have done her utmost to throw suspicion on him, although I think she regretted it later and, as for Shard, well, Mr Piper is everything which Shard is not – frank, athletic, good-looking, and (more than this) very attractive to two *tall* women, Niobe Nutley and Elysée Barnes. Shard was once engaged to a girl whom unkind acquaintances referred to as his "beanstalk". He broke off the engagement in consequence.'

'Poor little runt!'

'Pity is *not* akin to love, especially when it is couched in *those* terms.'

'Sorry. But I am truly sad about him, same as I am about Billie Kennett.'

'Billie Kennett? Ah, yes. The devil-marks on Elysée Barnes's fair body were the last straw, I think. She got the truth out of Elysée and brooded on it until she was ripe for murder. Ah, well, she has been faithful to her Cynara – in her fashion.'